Pride Publishing books by Matthew J. Metzger

Single Books
Best Behaviour
Enough

Starting Over
The Divorce
The Other Man
The Wedding

Starting Over

THE WEDDING

MATTHEW J. METZGER

The Wedding
ISBN # 978-1-83943-849-3
©Copyright Matthew J. Metzger 2020
Cover Art by Erin Dameron-Hill ©Copyright February 2020
Interior text design by Claire Siemaszkiewicz
Pride Publishing

Published in 2020 by Pride Publishing, United Kingdom.

Pride Publishing is an imprint of Totally Entwined Group Limited.

THE WEDDING

Dedication

For Danii

Chapter One

The seatbelt sign went out and Aled's phone went on.

Usually, Aled liked work sending him to the California office. They gave him a company credit card, paid for a nice hotel and the meal allowance was obscene. He always came back two stone heavier than when he left, and last time he'd been sent — only for a week — he'd come home to a boyfriend itching out of his skin for a good, hard fuck.

But six weeks was just taking the piss.

Six weeks of a staggering time difference, obscene heat and no sex. He felt grimy from the long flight, fat from the rich food and disconnected from his own partner. He wanted to see Gabriel. He wanted to shower. Then he wanted to completely undo the shower's hard work and fuck Gabriel until it hurt.

Hence the immediate turn to his phone.

It started to trill as the plane reached the gate and Aled thumbed through several updates from Suze, mostly asking why the flight was so late and demanding to know if he was screwing with her and was already at home, to finally — *finally* – find one from Gabriel.

Tea in the microwave, see you soon :) xx

Aled frowned. Tea in the microwave? So what? They could take a takeaway or make something at ridiculous o'clock in the morning and fuck on the kitchen floor like a couple of drunk teenagers.

Landed, Aled replied, despite the hour. *You all right? Have you come to meet me?*

Silence. Aled fidgeted. Gabriel was probably just — just waiting or something. Playing a game on his phone. In the toilets taking the edge off before Aled got there. There were many reasons he'd not instantly reply. It wasn't like flights were ever bang on time these days and getting through border control always took some time. He might even still be getting off the train at the airport station. It was fine.

Maybe.

He felt antsy anyway. He could tell himself that everything was fine all he wanted, but — but he didn't *know.* Gabriel was quiet. And Suze was noisy. Something was up.

So he hurried, jostling past other passengers to get off the plane as quickly as possible, near-running along the corridor to border control, muttering obscenities at the e-gate when it rejected his passport twice, jogging to baggage control, swearing the whole time under his breath waiting for his suitcase to appear…

Something was *wrong.*

It paid off. He was first out of the arrivals gate, scanning the crowd for that ink-black hair and devastating smile before he'd even cleared the automatic doors. And without the crowd having gathered sufficiently, he found a familiar face with no effort whatsoever.

Only it wasn't Gabriel.

It was Suze.

"Welcome home!" she cheered, holding out her arms for a hug.

Aled frowned, glancing around. She was on her own. Was he waiting to jump out from behind a pillar like a daft sod or something? Was he—

"No Gabriel?"

She huffed. "Good God. Hug me first."

"Where's Gabriel?"

Had he just not come?

"Hug! Now!"

Aled sighed and hugged her, before stepping back and demanding to know again.

"I bullied him into letting me come instead."

Aled relaxed a little. Suze was a force of nature. If she'd asked to come instead, and asked enough times, then she'd have worn Gabriel down.

"Why?"

"Because I wanted to see you," she said. "Anyway, he couldn't get out of work today and was fussing about not making it on time because of your early flight, so— ta-da! Am I not enough?"

"No offence, Suze, but I was looking forward to a bit of fun and you're not it."

"Gross," she drawled. "Well, I beat him in a fight, so suck it up. He'll be at home when we get there. Or still at work if we hurry. So how was San Diego?"

Aled whinged and told her all about the fiasco as he followed her to the exit for the car parks. The timing had been shit. Gabriel had only moved in with Aled about six months ago, and they'd been gearing up to go house shopping and find somewhere more *them*, rather than the house Aled had originally bought with his ex-wife. Then, the day before their first house-viewing appointments, Aled had been sent to America. In corporate terms, there had been a complete disaster. The head of marketing had been caught with his hand in the till, so to speak, and was being investigated for fraud in the millions of dollars. Which left a large company with dead weight, a mutinous building full of corrupt employees and nobody to train up their replacements.

And so Aled had been parachuted out there.

He'd tried to refuse. They'd offered a bonus *and* a raise, but he'd not wanted to go. It had taken months for Gabriel to stop being twitchy about living together — Aled hadn't wanted to throw their plans up in the air now they'd finally settled down.

But it had been Gabriel who'd told him to go.

'With that money, you could pay off the mortgage,' he'd said. *'We can get somewhere really nice, instead of having to settle. Go. It's not like I'll be all on my own.'*

Aled didn't mind. They had an open relationship by mutual agreement, although Aled rarely indulged. Gabriel called him emotionally monogamous, and it was true. Aled had never really been capable of loving multiple people at once. He got too focused on one person. But sex? Sex was different. He could have sex with multiple people guilt-free, and occasionally had since meeting Gabriel almost three years ago.

But Gabriel wasn't wired the same way. Sometimes he'd find a one-night stand on Grindr. Sometimes he'd sleep with the same man for weeks on end, then it would be over. And sometimes he had other relationships — other dates, other boyfriends, other partners. He'd been with Kevin since before he met Aled. Chris had been a regular topic of conversation for a couple of months. And Greg had been a weekly occurrence since July, although Aled could happily do without that twat within a hundred miles of him. *God, the man was a knob.*

But by and large, Aled didn't mind the presence of other men in their lives. As long as they treated Gabriel right and didn't interfere with his relationship with Aled, Aled was fine with it. The only real rule between them was honesty and Gabriel had always been unfailingly honest about his liaisons.

Still, if Gabriel had been screwing that shithead Greg in Aled's house...

"I'm guessing," Suze said as they reached the car, "that you want to go straight home and check up on the Archangel Gabriel?"

"I wouldn't call him that to his face."

"I did. He threw a pan at me."

"You deserved it, then."

"I did not!"

Aled snorted, settling into the passenger seat with a tired groan. "You did. And yes, incidentally. I've missed him."

"He's fine. He came over for Sunday dinner with us a couple of weeks ago. He's been taking the opportunity to hit up the biking trails a bit more without you."

"Oh my God, the conservatory floor —"

"Drama queen," Suze said snidely as she slid into the driver's seat. "He's had some friend over. Craig?"

"Chris?"

"That's it!"

Aled subsided, mollified. Chris was all right. He'd never actually met him face-to-face, but he called fairly frequently and Gabriel had been on the odd proper date with him. They'd met at some cycling event or other. Nutters.

"We didn't see him at all last week. He went off mountain biking in Snowdonia. Who cycles up a mountain?"

"Gabriel does," Aled groused. "He can't stay still for twenty seconds. I don't tie him up for the thrill. I tie him up to keep him in one place *long* enough to fuck him."

Suze laughed, peeling out of the car park and into the darkness. "Lies."

"Half-lies."

"Complete lies, I know you better than that." Then, oddly, her face sobered. "Um. So...he was going to come and meet you, but I asked if I could. I need to talk to you."

"Er...okay?"

There was a long silence.

"Um. Suze? Talking?"

"Oh. Yeah."

Another silence. Dread inched up Aled's spine.

"Suze—"

"I just—oh, fuck it."

Quite suddenly, she swerved over to the side of the road, and switched the hazard lights on. Aled blinked, startled, as she sat back and huffed at the steering wheel like it had offended her.

"Suze? Everything all right?"

"Yes. No. I don't know."

Aled frowned. Suze never didn't know. She was the epitome of going for it, no matter what it happened to be, and having no regrets.

"What's up?" he prompted softly.

"Tom's —"

Aled took one of her hands off the wheel to squeeze it. "Come on, Suze," he coaxed. "Talk to me."

"I don't know what to do," she said miserably. "On the one hand, it's everything I ever wanted, it's exactly where I want us to be going, it's what the end game's been ever since I was little, but — but it means —"

"Context? Please?"

She took a deep, shaking breath, and her face twisted like she was going to cry. "Tom's proposed."

Aled — blinked.

For a moment, his brain struggled with the words. He knew what they meant. Or, rather, he knew what they *should* mean. Congratulations. Celebrations. Several parties, a wedding, speeches, cake, eyeing her speculatively to see if there was a possible bump under the sleek white folds of the dress —

So why did Suze look like she wanted to punch the horn?

"My instinct," Aled said slowly, "is to congratulate you on the love of your life wanting to marry you, but you don't look like you want to be congratulated."

Aled and Suze had been best friends since they were in nursery school together. Growing up, Suze had had a tendency to date complete shits, and Aled had dutifully loathed every single one of her boyfriends until mild-mannered Tom had appeared on the scene when they were all in university. He wasn't the brightest spark in the world. He tended to open his mouth only to put his foot in it, and he and Gabriel had gotten off to a very bad start when Tom had made some extremely ignorant remarks, but he never meant ill by anything. He was — *nice*. It was the only word to really describe Tom. *Nice.* Laid-back, affable, friendly, loyal — and nice.

Tom and Suze had been together for almost fifteen years, and Aled was a little lost as to why Suze looked so upset at a proposal. He was a little surprised Tom *had* proposed — why bother, Aled figured, after a decade and a half — but why would Suze be annoyed about it?

"What's the problem?" he asked gently.

"I don't know."

"You don't know if you want to marry him?"

"No," Suze whispered. "I know I want to marry him. But — "

Aled waited, squeezing her hand.

And finally, there it was. "He wants us to start a family."

"You always wanted that too, didn't you?"

"Yes," Suze whispered, "but he was always so firm — we agreed — "

"Agreed what?"

"That they'd be near their family."

And the truth dawned on Aled in a rush.

Suze, with an estranged father she hadn't seen in twenty years, a brother in prison who wouldn't be out in *another* twenty years and a dead mother. Versus Tom, with an entire county covered in various siblings, cousins, aunts, uncles and grandparents.

"He's going home," Suze whispered. "He's going back to Cornwall to work for his dad's company now Jed's retiring — and he wants me to go too."

"Oh," said Aled. He sat back in his seat and frowned at the windscreen. "Right."

Suze simply sniffed loudly.

"You love him."

"Yes," Suze mumbled.

"You've loved him from the minute you saw him."

"Yes."

"And you're always going to love him."

"Yes."

"Then you say yes."

Her lip wobbled. "But that means leaving *you.*"

"I can't stand between you and the life you always wanted, Suze."

"It's not a life I want without you!"

"You're not going to be without me," he soothed, squeezing her hand over the tabletop. "I've known you since we were in nursery, Suze. And you've *always* wanted your own family. A real family. A better family than the one you started out with. And with Tom, you can have that. You can have the husband who loves you, not the one that runs out on you for a teenager. You can have the kids that grow up with a good future and good parents, not with one mad and one missing. They'll have grandmas and aunts and lots of cousins to play with out there. They won't need to squirm their way into some other kid's family on the same estate and pretend they were left on the wrong doorstep by the stork."

"But they won't have their Uncle Aled," Suze croaked.

Aled laughed. "'Course they will. This isn't the fifties, Suze. We can Skype and see each other still. I can drive down to visit. We could come for Christmas, me and Gabe, every year if you want. And summers! You'll have better summers in Cornwall than what we get here. All you have to do is tell Gabriel he can go cycling up a cliff or some such bollocks, and he'll drag us both down every year without fail."

Suze's lip started to shake again.

"Suze," Aled breathed, cupping her hand in both of his. "I love you. I *love* you. I've always loved you. You're the best friend I've ever had, you're the sister I never *did* have, and this is your future, your *happiness*, calling for you. Tom has *always* said he would be going home one day. He can't abandon his family, even for you—"

"I'd be abandoning—!"

"—and you can't abandon everything you ever wanted for me."

She burst into tears and Aled groaned, leaning over to hug her.

"If I could have loved you like I did Melissa, like I do Gabriel, then I would have done, and I would have lamped Tom the minute you saw him and removed the Cornish competition," he said, pressing his nose against her hair when she laughed wetly. "But we were never like that, Suze. We both knew this was going to happen eventually. You've always wanted your family, and for that to happen, you have to leave me behind a little."

"Not like this," she sobbed.

"Yes, like this," Aled coaxed. "Because Tom's *yours*. I never once got jealous of him. He took you away from me, he took my place as the most important man in your life, but I never once resented him because of how you looked at him. You absolutely adore him, Suze, and he's so besotted with you that I'm not even worried he'll fuck it up and I'll have to break his legs."

"Oh please, he'd kick your fat ginger arse," she mumbled.

"You forget how much effort I have to put into getting Gabriel pinned down. I'm a better fighter than I look, thank you."

"Yeah, and Tom plays rugby."

"Fine, point taken, but I'd still take a sledgehammer. See him beat that," Aled scoffed, squeezing her tightly. "Thing is, Suze, you will always, *always* regret it if you let him go because of me."

"I don't want to let *you* go," Suze insisted, fisting a hand into his jacket. "You're the only family I've got left, Aled. When your dad died, it was like *my* dad died. Nana is *my* nana. You're my brother, and my kids deserve you too, not just Daz and Gary and Neil and Jamie."

"Fuck me, how many brothers does Tom have!"

"Seven. And two sisters."

"Jesus Christ."

"And six steps."

"Well, you'll never have to pay a babysitter," Aled quipped, rocking her when she just cried harder. "Hey, come on, Suze. This isn't leaving me behind. This is giving me a free holiday home for Christmas, and the ability to actually like your kids because I won't get kid-phobia if they're a few hundred miles away."

She sniffled, clinging tight, and whispered, "I don't know — "

"Forget about me," Aled advised. "Answer him based purely and simply whether or not you want to marry him and have kids with him. Then do what you need to do in order to get that, because that's always been your dream, Suze."

"A *dream*, Aled. This is reality."

"And your reality is offering you that dream."

"In Cornwall. Miles from my best friend. From *my* family."

"From your tiny family who can't give you that," Aled said frankly. "Distance isn't going to change us, Suze. If we can cope with my wife who never quite trusted you, and your boyfriend who has never made a secret of the fact he's not staying in Yorkshire forever, then we can cope with a long car trip to get to each other physically. And if you go to Penzance or Plymouth instead of some middle-of-nowhere village, direct train! It's a win-win situation."

"Why couldn't I have fallen in love with you?" Suze mumbled morosely.

"We'd kill each other. Plus, still no kids."

Suze hummed, pulling away and scrubbing at her face. Her eyes were bloodshot and her cheeks flushed.

"You're more than just a mate, and that's why I know we'll be all right," Aled said gently, tucking her hair behind her ear. "You and me, we're stronger than any of this. Most best friends drop down to casual after weddings and shit. You and me? We're for good. You've caught a bloke who trusts you, who loves you, who doesn't question why your best mate is a man and what you're up to with him. And I've caught someone who actively shoves me out the door to spend time with you and Tom when he wants to play with someone else."

Suze laughed a little, then swallowed. "You have to come visit all the time."

"Of course I will."

"Gabe too."

"I'll just show him some pictures of cute Cornishmen and he'll be booking the tickets," Aled promised.

"And — and you'd be their uncle. When we have kids. They'd know all about you, and you'd have to send presents and come and see them, and we'd come and see you…"

"Eh, I'll visit you. You can leave the kids at home when you come back here," Aled negotiated.

Suze nodded, then exhaled heavily and started rummaging in her pockets for tissues. "So you think I should say yes."

"I think you should chase what you want from your future and adapt what you've got now to fit it."

"Which means saying yes," she admitted quietly. "I do want to marry him. I do want his kids. I just — I guess I always told myself that he might change his mind and want to stay here to have them. But why would he? All his family are there. And he misses them every day, just like I'd miss you —"

"Do what's best for you and Tom. Because no matter what you choose, you're not letting go of me to get it," Aled said, squeezing her arm. "I'll be at the other end of the phone, just like always."

Suze took a deep breath.

"So, I guess I'm engaged. And moving. If."

"If?"

"If you do one thing for me."

"What's that?"

"You have to give me away at my wedding."

Aled blinked. "Suze —"

"I don't want my dad there. He's no business being there. Or my real brother. And I always planned in my head that your dad would do it, but — but as he's gone, I want you to do it."

Aled swallowed against the lump in his throat. "Okay," he agreed hoarsely. "Yeah. 'Course I will."

She hugged him, flinging her arms around his neck, and squeezed tightly enough to choke him.

If they both cried a little, neither of them cared.

Chapter Two

Gabriel coasted the bike to a stop and planted one exhausted foot on the rocky ground.

"Fuck," he gasped. "Holy *fuck.*"

Chris just grinned. His face was flushed red from a combination of the wind and the effort. He'd won their race — of course he had, the jammy bastard — and was sitting atop a stray rock, a half-empty water bottle dangling limply from his fingers.

"Check out the view," he said.

The Dales were spread out below them, splashes of green and brown under a deep blue sky. The sun was beginning to sink, and the blue was slowly inching towards purple.

"How far have we gone?" Gabriel asked.

"Twenty-eight miles."

"*Fuck.*"

"Two more," Chris said. "Then the last train home."

"I might just sleep out here," Gabriel said. He propped his bike against the rock and stole Chris' water bottle, draining it in three desperate gulps. Chris just watched, a smirk playing around his lips. A little thrill of achievement chased up Gabriel's spine. Chris could be so *serious* sometimes. It was almost exciting to wrestle a smile out of him.

"I wouldn't recommend it," Chris said and slid down from the rock. "Anyway, your boyfriend will want you back tonight."

Gabriel rolled his eyes.

"Technically," he said, easing his sore arse back onto the saddle, "aren't you both my boyfriends?"

Chris just pushed off and didn't answer.

They'd met at a race. Aled would drop Gabriel off sometimes with the bike, but that was as close as Gabriel had managed to get him to cycling. He hated it. With a passion that made Gabriel wonder if a bike hadn't bitten him as a child. So Gabriel usually went to races alone — and there had been Chris. Shy. Gorgeous deep voice that creaked and rasped its way out on the odd occasion he chose to speak. A habit of glancing at Gabriel's tits then looking away again hastily that made Gabriel laugh.

He was sweet. And Gabriel didn't do sweet very often. He didn't usually like it, so he'd been intrigued by the warm flush in his stomach — and elsewhere — when Chris had stammered out an invite for a drink after that fateful race. He'd chased it. He'd wanted to understand it.

He still wanted to understand it.

But Chris wasn't wholly helpful. He was quiet and not entirely comfortable with unpacking his thoughts in front of other people. So Gabriel just asked the questions to himself, and by and large didn't bother to ask them.

But chasing the dying light down the hill, he drew up alongside Chris and echoed his rhythm until it felt oddly like a very choreographed spin class rather than the most punishing trail in the Peaks, then leaned forward over the bars and snuck a peek at Chris' red face.

"So—"

"What?" Chris croaked.

"Aren't you both my boyfriends?"

Chris coughed. "Uh. I don't— Your other bloke won't—"

"Aled," Gabriel said for the thousandth time.

"Um. Yeah."

There was a short silence and Gabriel chuckled.

"He won't give a shit if you're my boyfriend or not, you know."

Chris' foot slipped on the pedal, and he wobbled.

"He knows I've got them."

Sort of. Kevin wasn't a boyfriend, and Greg was just a friend with nine-inch benefits, but the theory was all there.

"Sure," Chris said. "'Course."

Gabriel smirked.

"You know," he said conversationally as the track began to level out and head down towards the road, "you could always stay the night and get the morning train."

"Work," Chris grunted.

"Next time, then."

"Um."

"You should meet him."

Even in the dying light, Gabriel could see the flush rapidly recede. He burst out laughing and almost came off.

"Oh my God, your *face*!"

"Shut up!" Chris whined.

"Aled works in marketing. Even if you were the other man, what's he gonna do? Throw a leaflet campaign at you?"

"Shut *up*!"

"You'd like him," Gabriel said as they wrestled the bikes over the bank and onto a narrow lane framed by tall hedges. They paused to get their bearings, then headed east for the nearer station. "You both think I'm crazy."

"You are."

"Well, yeah, but you both love me anyway."

Chris mumbled something that might have been a weak denial. Gabriel blissfully ignored it. He hooked a foot up onto the frame and coasted for a while, enjoying the cool evening. A harsh winter was approaching, and there'd be no more cycling for a while. Not beyond his commute to work, anyway. And sliding down Dewsbury Road in the ice after an eight-hour shift mopping floors and hoovering carpets wasn't anyone's idea of fun, least of all Gabriel's.

He dropped back a little to admire the view as they climbed the last hill, then winking village lights came into view. They managed the station with only seconds to spare and heaved the muddy bikes onto the train under the unamused nose of an elderly guard who'd fallen out of some costume drama on the telly. He sniffed at them for daring to actually have tickets, and Chris pulled a face as they leaned up against the partitions, bracketing the dirty bikes between them.

"You'd think we were delinquents."

"I am. Dunno about you."

"Someone has to be sensible here."

"Nah," Gabriel said, and cocked his head. His smile dimmed to a fond scrutiny of Chris' still-blushing face. "I can't figure you out, you know."

"Huh?"

"You asked me out the day we met, you booked those gig tickets after a week and you must text me every week with new trip ideas —"

Chris' skin flamed red again. "I...I like spending time with you."

"And I never hid Aled from you, and you're not bothered by him *existing*, but you're so sure he'll take one look at you and try and kill you."

Chris scuffed his shoe against the train floor.

"Something you want to tell me?" Gabriel pushed gently.

"Nah," Chris said. "Just — you know. Lots of guys *say* their boyfriends are okay with it."

"You're okay with it."

Chris frowned. "Huh?"

The carriage was empty. The guard had vanished into the next one. The train lurched through the darkness towards Sheffield, like they were the only two people in the world and civilisation was thousands of miles away. In that cocoon, Gabriel reached out and hooked his fingers around Chris' until the connection swayed between them in the gentle rocking of the carriage hurtling through the twilight.

"I've had a day out with my boyfriend," Gabriel murmured. "Now he's going home, and I'm going to see if my other boyfriend is home from the US yet."

Chris coloured faintly. He ducked his head, but not fast enough to hide the smile that flashed across his face.

"You're my boyfriend, and you don't mind the others," Gabriel said. "So why wouldn't Aled be like you?"

Chris opened his mouth, but there was no reply.

"I like people like you," Gabriel said. "Is it so surprising you have some things in common?"

"I — guess not."

"You've got loads in common, really."

"Like what?"

"Neither of you are what you look like."

Aled looked about as savage as a cabbage but liked to force Gabriel to his knees and fuck his face until he choked. Chris, with his shaved head, broken teeth and hard, stocky frame, looked like he could kill with a single punch but was about as aggressive as…well, the exact same cabbage. He didn't do kink. He didn't do rough sex. He barely even did *gentle* sex. They'd met at the beginning of the summer, and Gabriel had had him exactly twice. *Twice.* That had to be a record.

"I was expecting someone more…hard-looking," Chris admitted.

"Yeah, well, he's not."

"So you say."

"Meet him and you'll find out."

"No thanks."

Gabriel rolled his eyes. "Fine. You also both dip your biscuits in your tea wrong, and neither of you know how to match socks."

"Excuse me, I do *not* dunk wrong."

"You're supposed to dunk a *bit* of the biscuit, eat it then dunk a new bit. Not drown the whole thing then act surprised when it dissolves."

"It only dissolves if you used a shitty rich tea."

"Custard creams dissolve."

"Since when? Where the hell are you buying your custard creams?"

"And," Gabriel interrupted loudly, dropping Chris' hand, "you both let yourselves get drawn into dumb arguments about biscuits."

Chris snorted. He stepped forward as lights flickered outside and the train began to slow, and caught Gabriel's hip in one hand. If Aled was soft edges and fuzzy lines, Chris was forged out of steel. Even his hands felt hard, and the kiss grazed even as there wasn't a hint of demand in it. Gabriel melted a bit around the edges. God, he hoped he could persuade Chris into a proper fuck soon.

"Your fault," Chris muttered.

"Everything's my fault."

"True."

"Hey!"

"You said it, not me."

The debate was punctured by arriving into a quiet station. Gabriel followed Chris to the train bound for Bristol, but there were a couple of drunks on the platform, so he didn't quite dare to kiss him. Instead, they shared a back-thumping hug and a cheery, obnoxiously deep goodbye, before Gabriel hefted up his bike and headed for the shuttle that would wind its way towards Leeds, via Wakefield.

The text came in before he got there, though, and he grinned stupidly at the display.

Chris: Love you too xxx

"Softie."

The last train to Leeds was even lonelier than the last one in from the Peaks and Gabriel propped the bike against the trackside doors and flopped into a nearby seat to text Kevin. It wasn't a line he'd been giving Chris. Gabriel had only tried monogamy once and it had *really* not worked. He wasn't built for the same guy and the same sex over and over again — and he wasn't really built that way romantically, either. He wasn't in love with Kevin and certainly not with Greg, but he loved Aled to bits, and was rapidly heading that way with Chris too.

And how lucky was he that he had four guys who just...*got* it?

Okay, Chris was a work in progress. But Aled had always understood. So had Kevin. And Greg, okay, Greg didn't get it, but Greg was only interested in a buddy he could fuck after gigs sometimes, not a relationship or anything. He didn't give a shit if Gabriel had one boyfriend or twenty, just so long as he could come out to play sometimes.

Kevin was either busy with a client, busy with the kids or busy fucking his wife. Gabriel sighed and switched over to a game for the rest of the journey, then stuffed the phone away and wrestled his aching legs under him as Wakefield shivered into view. It was a short downhill coast from the station to Aled's house, but to his burning thighs it felt like a thousand miles.

Then he paused on the corner, grinning.

He'd locked up and turned all the lights out when he and Chris had left that morning. But the landing light was on, a warm yellow glow peeking out through the slats in the blind.

Aled was home.

Chapter Three

Aled was woken by off-key singing in the shower and it had never sounded so beautiful.

That was the mark of having been away too long, he decided. Gabriel's singing was not only off-key, it showed no awareness of even knowing what a key was. It was more correctly described as godawful screeching, similar to the death throes of a savaged cat, and yet it drew Aled gently out of his dreams like a siren song.

He threw back the covers and went hunting.

Aled was thirty-five years old, overweight and ginger. He had to wear glasses if he wanted to see more than a foot in front of his face and if he ever blushed, he looked like someone had set him alight. And Gabriel —

Aled stripped naked, marched into the bathroom and opened the shower cubicle.

Gabriel was gorgeous. Twenty-six and looking more like nineteen, thanks to the eternal youth bestowed upon him by the combination of his assigned sex and his hormone replacement therapy. He was slim and sleek, fat beads of water hanging on eyelashes so black that they shimmered a dark blue in the LED lighting of their bathroom. His hair was like ink spilled over his scalp and his eyes were an arresting dark blue, like a clear sky at twilight. Dark lips, dark nipples and a dark cock almost hidden in the trimmed pool of matching darkness at his crotch were the only disturbances to the miles of alabaster perfection in front of him, and even Aled's fair skin looked tanned against Gabriel's as they touched.

He didn't say anything. His arousal was burning too close to the surface for a game, but his lust was too strong for something sweet and loving. He didn't want to worship or love. He wanted to fuck. He wanted to stake a claim. He knew exactly what Gabriel got up to while Aled was away and who else would have been buried to the hilt inside him recently.

Well, now it was Aled's turn.

He was crude about it, shoving his way inside with nothing by means of preparation or play. Gabriel was tight and hot around him, like a fist in a silk glove squeezing his dick to the brink of pain. Some other time — soon — Aled would go slow. Tie Gabriel down and fuck him wide open, leave marks all over his skin and words to burrow into his brain. Play a proper game. But faced with the sheer sensuality of his naked body in the shower after six weeks apart, Aled fucked him like a faceless doll, the sound of skin on skin more like slaps than sex. It was over as quickly as it began. The climax smashed into him like a sucker-punch and he left a savage bite in the back of Gabriel's shoulder. He drew blood and smacked the wound when he pulled out again.

"Turn around."

Gabriel turned on wobbly knees. Aled caught the back of his neck and dragged him into a hungry kiss. It was all teeth and tongue, and the slippery hands that raked through his hair were shaking. He was shuddering with pent-up lust and Aled smirked when he pulled back.

"You want to come too?"

"Yes."

Aled raised a single eyebrow.

"Yes, sir. Please. Sir."

"Go on, then."

"S-sir?"

"Get yourself off," Aled said. "Or don't—whichever suits you. But—"

He leaned it, and bit down on Gabriel's earlobe until the gasp of pleasure turned into a whine of pain.

"You're not getting out of this bathroom until you've welcomed me home. *Properly.*"

* * * *

Properly took time.

Aled really should stop having sex in bathrooms. His lower back was killing him by the time they were done, and he fumbled his way into jeans and a T-shirt. His dick ached a bit too, but it was worth it. And it didn't ache as much as Gabriel's arse after being bent over the sink and *drilled.*

"Do we *have* to go out?"

Aled smirked. Gabriel was lying on the edge of their bed, feet on the floor and body on the mattress. He'd wriggled into his briefs and unzipped skinny jeans, then given up. His bare feet were sensual on the lush carpet and his bare breasts tempting against the crumpled sheets.

"Sorry, but yes. Tom and Suze got engaged and want to celebrate and talk plans over lunch."

"Can't we do that some other time?" Gabriel whined. "You just got home."

"And you're not very surprised by the news."

Gabriel shrugged. He began to toy with his left nipple. He'd had it pierced a couple of months ago and the silver ring flashed in the sunlight pouring through the window.

"Tom told me he was thinking about it," he said.

"Ahh."

"I'd rather stay here and welcome you home again."

Gabriel's voice had dropped huskily, and Aled smirked. He stepped over Gabriel's legs, bracketing his thighs between Aled's knees, and leaned over. Gabriel's wrists felt fragile in his hands as Aled pinned them to the bed. The ring was cold metal over a hot breast and he sucked until Gabriel whined breathlessly underneath him. The nipple itself hardened. Aled's cock was too tired to do the same.

"When we get back," he promised, "I will strap you down and thoroughly explore every inch of you."

Gabriel bit his lip.

"I'd rather you played with me."

Aled raised his eyebrows, surprised.

"Kevin's away, and Chris and I aren't really there yet. And I don't think he does forceful. I wanted to be *forced.*"

Aled smirked. "Okay," he said. "When we get back, we'll play a game. Any game you like. But we really do need to go now and have lunch with them."

Gabriel sighed, but lifted his head for a quick kiss and rolled out from under Aled. The ring was hidden by a bra, and a black T-shirt was poured over his slender back, the fuck having either rendered him too sore for his binder, or too blissed-out to care. Aled turned ideas over in his head as to which game they could play. He wasn't in the mood for especially violent, but a painful fuck drove Gabriel just as wild. Maybe he could fist him or get the bigger toys out. The ring would hurt if he jerked that around, but it was dangerous playing too much with Gabriel's tits. He didn't want to trigger any dysphoria in the middle of a game.

He pondered as they locked up and Gabriel bounced into the car. The engine took a couple of tries to get going, six weeks of sitting idle in the garage having helped nothing. Gabriel dug out his sunglasses from the glovebox and looked positively gothic in his blacks as he played on his phone. Aled smirked. It was a pity that forcing him into a skirt would definitely trigger dysphoria, because shoving him into some tiny leather dress that barely hid a chastity belt would definitely make for a fun game.

"I thought Chris was coming to stay?" he asked as they joined the shopping traffic.

"He did. He went home from our race yesterday. He gets the train."

"Doesn't he drive?"

"He can't afford a car."

"Huh," Aled said. "What does he do?"

"Works in a bike shop."

"Of course he does," Aled drawled. Gabriel just chuckled. "What are you guys, anyway? Just fucking, or is it a more involved thing?"

"More involved," Gabriel said. "Though it's a bit tricky."

"Why?"

"Erm, well, I think he's still figuring himself out."

"Ah," Aled said.

"Yeah."

"Surprised you've kept carrying on with him, then."

Gabriel shrugged. "I don't know. He's — fun. I like him. We never ever talk about it, but — yeah. He's supposedly not into men. I'm not totally sure he's ever been into anyone before."

Aled winced.

"I don't really know what to do about it," Gabriel admitted.

"Does it make you feel bad?"

"Most of the time, I forget that's how he feels. But when I remember, it feels awful."

Aled whistled through his teeth. "You know I can't help with that."

"Yeah, I know. You can listen, though."

"Always."

Aled couldn't sympathise. He was bisexual. Always had been. He'd known it from the start. He'd been more wound up about what got him off than who got him off. Getting aroused by violent kink was scary. Getting aroused by any gender wasn't. He could see why Chris figuring out his sexuality might upset Gabriel, but he couldn't really understand *why* Chris had to figure anything out. Why wasn't it as simple as it had been for Aled? Why wasn't it just a case of shrugging, saying, "Huh. Go figure," and having some more sex to make sure?

"For the minute, I'm kind of ignoring it," Gabriel said. "I mean, he's not using me as an experiment or anything, so it's not *really* gross. I'm just — I don't know. Rolling with it. When it stops being fun, I'll dump him."

Aled laughed. "You all over, that. Could you dump Greg first, though? He's a prick."

"He's a laugh!"

They argued good-naturedly about Greg. He was a recent recruit from the gym where Gabriel worked, and—in Aled's opinion—was nothing but a vain, empty-headed moron dangerously obsessed with weightlifting. But he and Gabriel liked the same shit music and had fucked in a toilet at Leeds Arena when some godawful band had been playing, so Gabriel liked him. At least he wasn't a shithead like one of Gabriel's stalker exes. He was just…*urgh*.

"Nobody said *you* have to fuck him," Gabriel pointed out as Aled pulled up into the pub car park.

"Just as well, I think it'd turn me straight."

"He's lovely in bed. *Very* considerate."

"I didn't think considerate got you off."

"Anyone rimming you like Greg does would get you off, trust me."

Aled coughed a laugh as they got out, then the conversation was thoroughly derailed by Suze's yell from the picnic benches outside the pub doors. It was still very warm, despite September having arrived and the leaves steadily turning red and brown on the trees. Tom simply grinned sheepishly, but Suze was full of energy, yesterday's tears and worries forgotten. A ring gleamed on her finger and she showed it off proudly as they approached. Aled grinned right back, his heart swelling. God, it was good to see her happy.

"I said yes!" she shrieked.

"More fool you," Gabriel said, but hugged her anyway.

Aled rolled his eyes and called Gabriel a grump before getting his own hug. He twirled her before setting her down again.

"I'll get the drinks," he said. "Anyone want booze?"

Surprisingly, the happy couple refused. Gabriel was a recovering alcoholic. He'd been dry for years now, but Aled didn't drink with Gabriel around, so it made for a cheap tray of Pepsis, which they clinked together in a toast as if they were champagnes.

"Still time to back out, you know," Gabriel said.

Tom grinned. "Nah, I'm all right, thanks."

"You say that now…"

"Hey, I want to be a dad. Clock's ticking now, mate. And she's got good genes."

Gabriel sniggered. "She's not a horse."

"Good ankles, long legs—"

"*She* is right here," Suze said snidely. "You got a death wish, Lazarri?"

"Nope. I'm safe. You'd not lift a finger against your best mate's boyfriend."

Tom guffawed. Suze's scowl said he wouldn't be safe for much longer, and Aled smirked.

"Safe from her. Not so much me. Just wait until I get you home. It's going to be the footlong for you."

Tom choked on his drink.

"Now you broke the fiancé," Gabriel said disapprovingly.

"If you both don't stop it, you won't be invited," Suze sulked.

"Bollocks," Aled drawled. He got whacked with her purse for his cheek, and promised a thrashing when Gabriel just laughed at him.

"Serious faces on!" Suze commanded. "Wedding. So. You're both coming. End of story. Aled has to give me away and Gabriel has to horrify my stupid relatives."

"Er, why? I don't do weddings. Leave me out of this."

"They're all raging bigots. We'll have to get you a tie coloured like the transgender flag," Aled said.

A devious grin spread over Gabriel's face. It was hot as hell and Aled shifted uncomfortably.

"I'm not wearing some ugly tie," Gabriel said, "but I think I'm going to pass as much as possible and spend the whole wedding with my tongue down Aled's throat. Oh! Can I bring Chris and neck with him too? That'll *really* horrify them."

Tom snorted with laughter and called him a slag. Aled just smirked. Gabriel could be a right belligerent tart if he sensed disapproval and Aled was already looking forward to the show.

"Anyway, Gabriel, if you don't come, Aled might get a bit too friendly with one of the bridesmaids," Suze said.

Gabriel raised his eyebrows. "And I should care because…?"

"God, close your relationship already. It's too hard to blackmail you."

"Nope. It's an added bonus."

"I hate you both," Suze proclaimed dramatically, then completely ruined the moment by saying, "And you're both coming, so shut up before I have to break one of you and ruin the photos."

"When is it?" Aled asked.

"We were thinking April."

"And in Cornwall," Tom said. "But you'd both be part of the wedding party proper, so we can sort you out with somewhere to stay. I'm taking up part of my dad's business."

"Eh?" Gabriel said.

"Tom's dad owns a hotel chain," Aled supplied.

"Oh. *Oh.* Er, why haven't we taken advantage of this before?"

"I don't want to know what you two do in hotels," Tom said primly.

"Nothing," Aled said. "We've never stayed in a hotel together."

Cabins, tents, hostels, villas, caravans, that one time overnight in an airport—but no hotels. Not *together.*

Gabriel got up to plenty in hotels with other people, but not with Aled. And Aled had only got up to things in hotels back when he was married, with his wife, on holidays — like most husbands with a sex life — or when work sent him to the San Diego office and his British accent tricked someone in the local bar into thinking that he was sexy.

"Maybe we should," Gabriel said sweetly.

"Not in my dad's hotels!"

"Mm, a touch of the forbidden. I like it."

"You're both gross."

"And *you're* so vanilla there's something wrong with you," Gabriel said sweetly.

"Hey!" Suze clapped her hands with a deafening crack. "Focus! *Wedding*!"

"Okay, okay, we'll come to Cornwall." Gabriel rolled his eyes. "It's only a few hours away. Not the end of the earth."

Aled could have kissed him for the comment, after Suze's meltdown in the car. She bit her lip, a funny look coming over her face, then shook herself.

"Yeah. Well. Um. I need you on board before the big day too, you know. I need my best friend for pre-wedding stuff. And to shop dresses with me."

Oh, no. No-no-no-no. Aled shook his head at once. "I draw the line at dress shopping."

"Brother of the bride, you have to."

"Who's been married here?" Aled argued. "I don't. Women only at those things."

Suze's gaze flickered ever so slightly to Gabriel, who narrowed his eyes and said, "Don't even think about it," in a sharp voice.

"Then it has to be you, Aled."

"You need to get more female friends."

"I am *not* taking Jen dress shopping. Her taste is *awful —*"

"You had to say it, didn't you," Tom said accusingly then overrode the imminent rant by loudly declaring that he'd cause a family feud by which brother to pick for his best man.

"Pick a friend, then."

"That'd be even worse."

A waitress with menus interrupted the debate and it moved seamlessly to food. Tom was dismissed to the bar and Gabriel took the opportunity to go to the gents. Possibly he'd sensed Suze's fidgeting, for the minute both men were out of earshot, she leaned across the picnic bench towards Aled.

"I'm going to need you," she implored. *"Both* of you. Tom's mum is a right controlling cow and his dad is a bigot. It has to be exactly like this, this is how all Hoopers get married, blah blah blah. I want it to be *my* wedding, not whatever Tom's parents' wedding was like."

"Well, you know where to find me when you need a rant, but I draw the line at dress shopping," Aled said.

"I need your advice. Your wedding was amazing."

"Don't take wedding advice from the divorced guy," Aled warned.

She rolled her eyes. "I said *wedding*. Not *marriage* advice. You sucked at being married."

"True."

"But then, you and Melissa weren't right for each other in the end. You and Gabriel are."

Aled stiffened. "What?"

"You and Gabriel! Doesn't this make you want to do it again?"

"Right," Aled drawled and jerked his thumb over his shoulder at the pub doors. "You think Gabriel could say inside his suit long enough to get married? He'd go traditional and shag the best man."

"Excuse me, *I'd* be your best man, so no he wouldn't," Suze said tartly.

"Face it, Suze, I'm living in sin and I like it. I'm not getting hitched again."

"Fine," she said airily, waving a hand as though brushing his objection aside. "But you're making a mistake. You have something incredible in your lap — most of the time literally! — and you don't want to stake a claim? Stupid."

"Staked plenty of claims," Aled said blithely.

"Aled!"

Aled twisted around. Gabriel was hovering at the pub doors.

"I, er, I forgot my wallet," he said.

"S'fine," Aled said. "I'll get it."

He got the double meaning, too, when Gabriel loped over and leaned down to whisper in his ear.

"I'll owe you one."

Oh. *Oh.*

Aled nodded, feigning absent-minded ignorance, and patted his bum lightly. But the cogs had started to turn. He'd be staking another claim tonight and giving Gabriel that painful fuck he was after.

But other cogs were turning too.

About Suze's wedding words, the way Gabriel fit as he slid down to sit by Aled's side and cuddle up for a moment, and the empty space on Aled's third finger, still a shade paler than the rest of his hand from the gold ring he'd worn for years.

He hadn't thought about it since the divorce.

But —

Suddenly, it was there in the back of his mind like it had never gone away.

Chapter Four

"Ssh."

The hand that smoothed down his sweat-soaked spine was soft and warm. Kind. It had been harsh for what felt like forever, but now it was gentle. Gabriel dragged his consciousness around it, and tried to breathe past the blinding euphoria, the cold adrenalin and the throbbing pain.

"In."

He breathed in. The hand on his back rose with the effort.

"And out."

He exhaled. It sank.

"Good."

The praise was warm. He'd been good. He *felt* good.

"I'm going to untie you now. Just relax."

The rope had been rough and painful. It scraped. He whimpered as it scratched at sore skin, and the hand pressed down on his back again. Grounding him between its heavy weight and the firm mattress.

"It's okay. You're safe. Game over."

Game over.

The little jolt of security was like a lock turning in a heavy door to shut out the world. Like when he'd been living in the council flat and had slid the bolt home on the teenagers shouting at him in the hall, on the creepy guys who wanted to fix him, on the neighbour who'd called him a tr —

"Safe."

The sheet was cool cotton, soft and light. It washed over his naked legs and drifted up until he was covered to the shoulder. One by one, his strained limbs were released and tucked into the safe cocoon.

Safe. Safe.

"Aled."

The name was soft on his tongue. He blurred the last letter until it almost vanished. The kiss between his shoulder blades was chaste and calming. He breathed out and relaxed into the mattress. The pain dulled. The adrenalin soaked away into the sheets, leaving only the blissful haze behind.

He drifted.

Vaguely, he was aware of careful fingers rubbing cream into his skin, both inside and out. The brief sting was offset by the soft rub of a thumb in the small of his back, and soon it was over. The scent of massage oil was understated in the quiet room and it pooled in liquid heat right where he'd been kissed a moment earlier.

"How do you feel?"

He knew that question. The little ritual to draw him up from his headspace, or to bring him down from the high. If *game over* was the bolt on the door, then *how do you feel* was the bodyguard between him and the bolt. The great wall that blocked out the world. The Kevins, the Aleds, even the Chrises. The men who could smash him into pieces, who lived inside his armour, and yet would never cause a crack.

Gabriel curled his fingers into the pillow under his head and let out a long, *long* sigh.

"Safe," he whispered. "Loved."

There were many words—cared for, looked after, cherished, wanted, needed, secure, home, protected, defended, adored—but he only needed those two.

"How do I feel?"

He smiled, drunk on his drifting pleasure.

"You love me."

A kiss was pressed gently to the back of his neck as hands worked the oil into his skin. Knots eased. Tension from fighting, thrashing, screaming, begging, were eased away. Everything unlocked, and he dissolved into the same sea that cradled him on the gentle ebb and flow of an idle tide.

"I do."

The quiet cupped them like a shield and Gabriel dozed. In truth, he didn't much need the aftercare. They hadn't played the game in months, but it wasn't an especially violent one. It wasn't scary. It was just—

Aled paid for dinner and expected sex in return. Gabriel said he didn't want to. Aled would make him.

That was all. As far as their games went, it could be tame and simple, or violent and terrifying. And they had played it simpler. He had been tied down until he could barely wriggle, then Aled had fucked him without enough preparation, and with his underwear forced between Gabriel's teeth so he couldn't scream. No beatings, no whipping, no facefucking or painful toys. Just a length of rope and a hard dick. The verbal abuse had been the real kink, and—as always—it was Aled who needed the cooling-off period afterward.

Gabriel loved dirty talk, abusive talk, during sex. Aled…

Well, he liked doing it. Then afterwards, when it was over, he would get sick at himself for saying it—for *enjoying* it—and he would need to be looked after. These moments in the afterglow had always been more for Aled than for Gabriel.

Slowly, Gabriel rolled onto his back and beckoned. Aled folded down into the sheets beside him and Gabriel cuddled up, sleepily sliding his leg between Aled's and nestling against his chest. He could feel that low, gentle heartbeat. Feel it, not quite hear it. Feel it in the gentle flutter of skin against his palm.

"That was great," he murmured.

"Yeah?"

"Mhmm. Missed you."

A hand carded gently through his hair. The other landed on his arse, a thumb gently stroking over one cheek.

"I've missed you too," Aled murmured.

"Did you do it all vanilla-style in America?"

"Yeah."

"Boring."

Aled chuckled. "Well, it took the edge off. But yeah. It was a bit boring. What about you? Is Chris into all sorts of weird shit?"

"Sort of." Gabriel yawned. "He's got issues, I think."

"Oh?"

"I don't really know. He doesn't like it if I respond much."

"If you *respond* much?"

"Yeah. Like—he'd like what you just did. Tie me down so I can't move or speak, and fuck me. But he doesn't like it otherwise."

"Huh," Aled said. "Do *you* like it?"

"Sure," Gabriel said, tugging on a couple of chest hairs. "Wouldn't let him do it if I didn't like it."

But in an odd sort of way, he didn't like it in the same way he liked...well, sex with other people. With Chris, it always felt oddly non-sexual. Like holding hands or hugging. His cock would move around inside, he'd come — probably — then he was done and throwing away the condom. He fucked like he needed to scratch an itch but didn't actually *like* having sex.

Gabriel liked to feel used sometimes. It was one of his little kinks. He liked to be just bent over the sink and fucked, or tie down and screwed, or even — though he'd never tell Aled, because Aled would hit the roof — to wake up in the middle of sex that had started without him. But he got the feeling that Chris wasn't exactly *playing* when he did it. That he really *was* using Gabriel's body as a means to an end, and that he was actually *with* Gabriel for all the other reasons to date someone.

Gabriel hadn't figured it out yet. He was ninety-nine percent sure that Chris hadn't figured it out yet either.

Maybe that was why he tolerated Chris needing to figure it out more than he ever had with anybody else.

"When does Kevin come back from holiday?"

Gabriel was jerked from his musings by Aled's question.

"Sorry?"

"You said Kevin's away. When does he get back?"

"Next week. Why?"

Aled's fingers drummed lightly on Gabriel's upper arm. "Been a while since he sent me a new video."

Gabriel smirked. "I'll text him in the morning."

"Hmm. Maybe."

"Maybe?"

"I've got the week off."

"So?"

"So that was nice and all, but—" Blunt nails scratched lightly at Gabriel's hair. "It was just for starters."

Gabriel closed his eyes and slid his arm across Aled's stomach. He buried his nose against a light dusting of chest hair and sighed as the soft cushion under his frame relaxed.

"I look forward to it," he muttered.

The light pat on his backside was promising—but, right now, Gabriel had no desire for more.

* * * *

Aled went off to see his nana later in the day, and the first that Gabriel knew of it was a deeply unimpressed voice coming from the conservatory door.

"I hope you're going to clean up after yourself this time."

Gabriel glanced up over the upended bike and grinned.

"Hello to you too."

"I *mean* it."

"Yeah, yeah."

Aled grunted but dropped into the wicker chair in the corner.

"How's Nana?"

"She's fine. Think the dementia's starting to speed up, but she's still pretty with it. Told her that Suze is getting married, but she seemed to think *I* was getting married."

Gabriel laughed. "Again, or your first wedding?"

"First one."

"What was that like?" Gabriel asked curiously.

Aled shrugged. "Church, posh hotel, ridiculous amount of flowers. Ridiculous amount of *money*, but Melissa's dad paid for most of it."

"Why?"

"Melissa was the golden girl. Her older sister was a complete nightmare. I think her dad was just pleased one of them turned out all right."

Gabriel chuckled. "Can't relate."

"Your dad not have a favourite?"

"What dad?" Gabriel quipped. "Just had a mother. And I was definitely not the favourite, even before I turned out to be a man."

"Ah."

"I don't think I've ever been to a wedding," Gabriel mused. He rolled his tongue around his teeth as he adjusted the freshly oiled chain.

"What about Kevin's?"

"No, they ran away together. Nobody went."

"Nice," Aled said approvingly. "What brought that on?"

"I think Kevin just wanted to piss off his mother-in-law, to be honest," Gabriel said. "Why did you get married?"

"It's what I grew up with," Aled admitted. "You love someone, you marry them. It's what you do. And I loved Melissa, so I married her."

"Huh."

Aled shrugged. "It felt natural to do it. I did want to, despite how everything turned out. I absolutely adored her. Why wouldn't I marry her?"

"Charming," Gabriel said.

"Eh?"

"You've never asked me."

Aled barked a laugh. "Yeah, well, I learned from the last time. Anyway, it was hard enough just to get you to move in."

"True."

"You ever see yourself getting married?"

"Nah," Gabriel said. He righted the bike and propped it by the door. "Waste of time and money, and just creates a load of drama. Why bother. I'd not even bother going to Suze's if she'd not kill me for skipping out."

"Damn right she will."

"At least I get to sleep with the best man," Gabriel said, wiping off his hands on a rag and eyeing Aled from head to toe. "You going to wear a *proper* suit, instead of your office gear?"

"Yeah. Waistcoat and pocket watch and all."

"Ooh, à la *Downton Abbey*."

"More or less."

It was a very nice mental image. Gabriel had guessed when they first met at Aled being the type who liked to pretend to fuck interns and secretaries, but it had never come out in any of their games. And to be honest, Aled's work suits weren't the best look on him. They didn't fit well, and his ties were ugly as sin. Gabriel had standards, after all. He wasn't getting tied up with paisley.

But a wedding suit might be different. A wedding suit might be—

"Vanilla fuck in a toilet while the bride and groom are dancing, or something more...sinister?"

Aled snorted. "It's you. If I did fuck you vanilla, you'd be begging for more in minutes."

"You don't always give it to me, though."

"Usually because you don't deserve it."

"I always deserve—"

He caught his words when Aled raised a single eyebrow and very abruptly shoved a hand down the front of Gabriel's briefs. It was hot and hard, gripping him like a vice, and it didn't take more than a quick wriggle to get one of those rough fingers inside him. Gabriel bit his lip and very slowly squeezed.

"You were about to tell me what sluts deserve?" Aled asked softly.

Game on.

"Don't call me a slut, you son of a bitch," Gabriel whispered and jutted out his chin.

The finger pushed deeper. A murmur across his jaw asked for a colour. A thumb probed at his thickening cock, teasing it out from the labia.

"Green."

Game-fucking-on.

Chapter Five

Aled woke to the rain.

It was dark, the clock on the side reading four-twenty-four, and the hammer of water on the conservatory roof below the window deafening.

Sighing, Aled decided to give up on trying to sleep. It was simply too loud and he had a vague need to piss. Sliding free of the sheets, he felt his way blindly to the door, then slipped out onto the landing and switched on the bathroom light.

It was chilly—he'd left the bathroom window open again—and goosebumps rose under the freckles as Aled pissed and washed his hands. Eyeing himself critically in the mirror, he decided to up the swimming to seventy-five laps a session, then retreated to the bedroom. He needed his dressing gown, at the very least. He'd not get back into bed, because then he'd wake—

But inching back into the bedroom stopped all his good intentions.

The light spilling in from the landing cast a gentle glow over the bed. Gabriel had twisted onto his back, the sheets pushed down to his waist, and his alabaster chest rose and fell in soft breaths. His eyelashes were a fan of darkness cast over his face. And that face — that perfect, peaceful face — was turned towards Aled's empty spot, long neck exposed, as though inviting a touch, a kiss, a comfort.

As though he missed Aled, even in sleep.

Aled's chest seized up tight. For a moment, there was no air. There was nothing at all but the fist around his heart, squeezing every drop of blood from it — and unable to empty it. Because nothing, *nothing,* could dislodge what Aled felt.

He closed the door with a snap.

In the darkness, the sheets rustled. Aled followed the sound, crawling up onto the bed and tugging the duvet down and away. Gabriel's skin was hot and soft and Aled spread his fingers as though to catch it. Stroking it. From knee to thigh, across the flat plains of belly and chest, sliding up lean arms as he pressed down, spreading his weight and sinking into the heat as though into a hot bath, until his lips found neck, jaw, cheek — *lips.*

Movement. A stir, quickly soothed. A word against his mouth, but Aled didn't hear it. Fingers ghosted across his ear, but he caught them and set them down again.

"Let me."

A soft sigh was his only reply, and Aled began to kiss where his hands had explored. Without sight, he could still see. He knew this body, this man, well enough to find the scars in the dark and smooth them over with lips and tongue. He could find the freckles without feeling them and he could kiss the lines of muscle too relaxed to be touched. He could press his face to ribs and hips, feel blood and breath and *life*, that brilliant, beautiful, bloody-minded *soul* that burned Gabriel bright from the inside out.

Aled could touch it all, in the dark silence of their bed.

He settled for the longest time, simply touching. There was a hedonistic pleasure in this. Gabriel was so lively, so stunning, that it was often difficult to touch him without it either leading to more, or being disrupted by his energetic need to be doing something else. And with his skin hot with sleep, it was like touching a living example of luxury. Aled could feel the idle flow of blood in hidden veins and he could feel the wash of air every time Gabriel breathed. He found himself kissing in time to that breathing, stroking his lips along Gabriel's jaw to catch his own with every sigh. And when Gabriel tried to nip, Aled teased himself free. When Gabriel tried to clutch, Aled smoothed the grip away again.

"Let me," he repeated, his voice barely audible in the dark, and Gabriel relaxed into the cushions. His hands drifted up to clutch at the pillows, and Aled kissed each elbow in turn before making his way down them, layering the skin with soft touches, fingers and mouth. He pressed attention into the marks he'd left around Gabriel's throat. He tasted the skin of his collarbone and soothed the invisible nicks where he'd twisted his nails against his nipples. For the longest time, Aled rested his lips against the gentle thud, buried deep beneath the skin of Gabriel's chest and breathed.

Simply breathed.

Breathed Gabriel's heartbeat. Breathed his smell. Breathed his warmth and the rise and fall of his ribs.

Breathed, and felt the hairs on his chest shift with every one. Then, as he felt Gabriel's heart begin to slow, Aled resumed his path, kissing down Gabriel's breastbone to his belly.

There was Aled's favourite place to rest. Slim did not mean steel, and he rested his head against the downy hair of Gabriel's stomach and relaxed, his hands taking over his exploration. Gabriel's breathing made Aled's head shift in gentle swells, like lying in a hammock or being at sea, and Aled relaxed, riding the tide in the dark, as he smoothed both hands around hips and thighs, creating patterns in the hair, until he found his mark.

His dry mark.

Aled kissed the edge of a hip and broke from the warmth long enough to find the bottle of lubricant in the bedside table. Gabriel stirred a little at the pop of the cap, then let out a breathy murmur as Aled began to massage it over his cock and inner thighs, then whimper as the prickling heat began.

"Nope," Aled whispered, catching a hand that tried to come down and returning it to the pillow. "All mine."

He saved this lubricant for special occasions. It tingled and burned — Aled liked the feel of it well enough, but it drove Gabriel absolutely crazy. And as Aled spread it over hot skin, Gabriel shifted restlessly, and whimpered as Aled explored inside as well as out. Silken heat gripped his fingers. A shiver rose past his mouth as he kissed Gabriel's stomach — the same as always. There was dryness, and a tension at odds to the languid beauty of Gabriel's limbs, but as Aled massaged and coaxed, both were soothed away, until

Gabriel was uttering little gasps with every breath, and his legs were shifting restlessly at Aled's sides.

"Now," he whispered. *"Please."*

"Ssh," Aled soothed, and tracked his mouth lower. Gabriel's cock burned against his tongue, and he teased it between his lips rather than truly sucking it. The pleasure that swept over Gabriel seemed to shred him, leaving him shuddering and dazed under — around — Aled's hands.

Only then did Aled press the tip of his cock inside.

The grip was far tighter than usual, thanks to the residual pain of their earlier game, and Aled paused less for Gabriel and more for himself. The urge was to simply thrust past it, to force his way in as he had countless times — and with less preparation — before. But he fought it, closing his eyes and pressing his lips to Gabriel's breastbone to ride out the intense heat and the buzz of the lube. He was beginning to regret that choice…slightly.

He pushed forward in slow increments, bracing his weight on the mattress and feathering kisses over Gabriel's heaving chest as he moved. Only once he was buried to the root did he shift down onto his elbows and kiss and knead with his teeth at Gabriel's neck, finding a shivering pulse and worshipping it idly until the incredible pressure began to ease, and the tension in the body beneath him ebbed away.

And he remained still, completely still, until Gabriel whispered, "Please."

Aled preferred long strokes, hard and bed-shaking. But this time, he simply rolled his hips, and *felt.* He could feel every inch of skin inside, every clutching muscle and every jumping nerve. The tightness was unnatural for Gabriel but the feeling of being buried inside him was not. It was like coming home, like he hadn't left the US until tonight, and Aled sank into it and him with hedonistic, utterly selfish pleasure.

"Can I—?"

Gabriel's fingers caught in his hair. His lips found Aled's in the dark, and his whisper was inaudible, yet somehow deafening.

So Aled pressed close, pressed as deep into him as possible, and came so hard that it rattled his bones, shaking his muscles loose like an hour in a Jacuzzi, pouring every bit of anxiety and hesitance away like worthless tat.

And even as he softened, he remained.

He simply curled around the heat in his arms, gathering skin and hair and *life* close to his chest, and relaxed.

He was home.

And everything was fine.

* * * *

He didn't get to keep Gabriel to himself the next day. Apparently, someone had to go to work. At the time, Aled had just turned over into the warm spot and ignored everything except that nice dream he'd been having but waiting up to an empty house four hours later was a bit of a downer.

Especially when he was woken by his phone ringing. Constantly.

"I swear to God…" he muttered.

Thinking it would be work, he dragged himself out of the nest to find it. His big mistake was not checking the caller ID before answering it, then his second was not hanging up on the shriek in his ear.

"Get up!"

"Urgh. No."

"Get up!" Suze insisted.

"Let me guess." Aled dragged himself back into bed and threw the duvet over his head. "You've said yes, and now you both want to go out and get pissed."

"Well, not *right* now. Actually, change of topic—"

She wittered on about needing to borrow his spare pump for a flat tyre, and Aled let the noise wash over him as he slowly woke up. He'd not slept especially deeply, but he felt drunk on being in his own bed again. And possibly having some decent sex for the first time in six weeks, too.

And other emotions.

"Suze."

"So I told him that—"

"*Suze.*"

"What?"

"I thought about what you said."

There was a short pause. Aled snorted with laughter.

"Okay, one specific thing you said. About me and Gabriel."

"What *about* you and—oh my God, no."

He waited.

"Are you really?"

"Just a thought," he said.

"But how serious is the thought?"

"Not very." Given that it had occurred somewhere around half-four in the morning, and Gabriel asleep was about as beautiful as he ever got because the sarcasm *stopped* for five fucking minutes.

"Aled."

"It was more what you said about my marriage."

Aled knew exactly why he'd ended up divorced. He'd married the most wonderful woman in the world—then forgot to let her know. Looking back, they'd been fracturing long before they'd found out he was never going to have children. The infertility might have been the breaking point, but if he'd kept paying enough damn attention, then Melissa would have loved him enough to stay.

He knew that now.

And Suze's little jab had him wondering less about marrying *Gabriel* and more about marrying at all. Would he make the same mistake again, now he knew what to look for? Would he still get lazy if he had another ring on his finger?

"Are you going to ask him?" Suze asked softly.

Aled smiled down at his bare fingers and clenched them into a loose fist. Gabriel would look good with a ring, but—

"Am I heck," he said. "All the effort I put in just to get him to move in with me? He'd run a mile if I proposed."

Except he probably wouldn't.

Chapter Six

Gabriel's phone lit up on the desk at exactly one minute to six.

He eyed it suspiciously for a moment, the timing just a little too perfect. He'd been on memberships all day, and he didn't remember telling Aled that, but the man always seemed to pounce on membership days. It was like he could just *sense* that Gabriel had spent all day sitting around doing nothing.

Gabriel worked at Aled's gym. He'd started just mopping floors and restocking the toilet roll in the bogs, but his chatty nature with the customers had earned him a promotion up to front of house, so to speak. The money wasn't great, but he liked the job just fine. And he liked being able to pay half the monthly bills and still having a little leftover to himself.

Gabriel had been homeless once. He'd left home at sixteen, and not entirely of his own volition. Now he had a home, and backup options should everything with Aled collapse around his ears, but the paranoia had never left him. He had an emergency fund that nobody else knew about, and he still carefully shaved a little off his wages every month to top it up. Just in case. *Just in case.*

Aled: Want to play tonight?

And the just in case was never more obvious than their games. After Gabriel had lost his job and moved in with Aled to avoid another go at homelessness, he'd lost the ability to enjoy some of his favourite games. Like Aled paying for a weekend at the beach and renting Gabriel as well as the holiday cottage. Some games, Gabriel thought sadly, were probably gone forever.

Then he shook himself and pushed up from the desk.

"I'm off, Caroline!"

"Have a good night, sweetie!"

He waved as he gathered his things, mulling over what to suggest. They hadn't played a rough game since Aled had gone to the USA, so it was seriously overdue. But where to start? If Aled was going to break this soft streak, then Gabriel wanted some mindfucking as well as just ordinary fucking. A bit of metal and leather wasn't going to cut it.

Me: What do you have in mind?

Aled: I'll think about it.

Gabriel rolled his eyes as he walked out into the unreasonably chilly carpark. It was threatening rain. His bike was damp as he unlocked it from the railings. It was going to be a —

A horn sounded.

A very familiar horn.

Gabriel grinned as the car coasted to a stop right in front of him, missing the front wheel of his bike by a hair's breadth. The tinted glass and white paint looked like something out of an advert, and the way the driver's-side window eased down to reveal the driver was a movie.

"Get in," Aled said.

Gabriel hooked the bike up to the back, then wandered around to the passenger side. Aled was in a predatory mood. The mirrored sunglasses and the lack of a kiss or friendly greeting said it all. Gabriel's blood began to head south in anticipation. He was going to be fucked in a field or a car park. Maybe even suck Aled off while parked up on a busy shopping street, only the black glass between him and a bunch of gossipy mums after the best bargains.

Or not. Aled took a seemingly aimless route out of Wakefield, heading north into Leeds. Passing Belle Isle was familiar, and Gabriel wondered for a wild minute if Aled meant to fuck him in his old flat building, but that, too, sailed past. The traffic was fairly calm, and it began to rain in earnest as Aled finally pulled off the main road into an industrial estate and stopped in a car park next to a brooding black warehouse of a building.

"Where are we?" Gabriel asked.

"The club."

Gabriel blinked. "A nightclub? You know that's a —"

"Not a nightclub," Aled said. "A fetish club. They don't even allow alcohol in here. You'll be fine."

Gabriel bypassed the alcohol issue entirely. Fetish club. A prickle ran up his spine. It was an odd mixture of fear and arousal. Kevin had taken him to one in

Manchester a few years ago, but for private sessions. Not — not just —

"Colour?"

Gabriel chewed on his lip. "I — yellow."

Aled's hand on his back was warm and soothing.

"Tell me."

"Are you a member here?"

"Yeah. Melissa and I went to their theme nights a few times. I think she had a bit of a nudist streak, to be honest. I've not been in years, though."

"What are we going to do in there?"

"I'm going to fuck you," Aled said simply. "And other people are going to see. That's it."

"They'll try and touch me."

He'd barely been able to walk through the one in Manchester without hands appearing out of nowhere to touch him. And Gabriel liked the idea of being shared out like a toy, but something had always stopped him. It was a shade too scary. A fraction too dangerous. He'd tried with Kevin those few times in Manchester, but had always chickened out at the last minute, too scared to relax and enjoy the truly anonymous fuck.

"They'll touch me," Gabriel repeated. "I can't. I like the idea, but I tried all of that and it's too scary. I can't do it."

The hand rubbed up his back once, and down again. Heavy. Hard. A comforting protection. He relaxed and the spike of anxiety bled away. It wasn't like Aled was going to make him do anything he didn't want to do.

"Nobody here is going to touch anyone without permission," Aled said quietly. "That's why we used to play here. They're strict. And there won't be permission—you'll not be doing any talking and I'm not going to be letting other people touch my things."

The cramp in Gabriel's gut eased. He took a deep breath.

"I want you naked, and I want to fuck you. But—"

"I want a blindfold."

Aled paused.

"I know they'll all be looking at me, but—I—can you blindfold me?"

Aled's fingers hooked behind his ear. The kiss was nothing like any of their games. It was soft and sweet and Gabriel relaxed into it.

"Okay," Aled murmured. "I'll show you where we're going, then I'll take you into the locker room, strip you off and blindfold you. Colour?"

"Green."

"All of them."

"Green for go. Yellow for pause. Red for stop," Gabriel recited.

"Good."

Then his thigh was slapped, the crack deafening in the quiet darkness of the car, and the next word was a hundred times harsher.

"Out."

Gabriel got out. It was raining heavily, but he waited anyway. Aled's hand slid into his back pocket and he was steered across the car park to a metal door with a CCTV camera staring down at them. Aled pressed an intercom button, said something about a membership and a guest, and a lock released. They were allowed into a featureless airlock and only once the metal door had locked again behind them did the inner door release.

Then Gabriel stepped into a luxury hotel.

At least, it looked like one. A roomy atrium, with a mahogany reception desk near the door and beyond it an array of fancy-looking sofas. It wasn't busy. Three or four couples were scattered about, talking quietly. A staircase disappeared into the floor in one corner, and a sign informed him that the changing rooms were somewhere to his right.

Aled spoke to the twinkly receptionist while Gabriel stared around. He was made to sign a rulesheet, then handed a towel and a locker key before Aled's hand returned to his back pocket and he was steered into the locker room. It was like the sauna in Leeds he'd been to a few times with some of his Grindr playthings. Warm, dark and close.

"Clothes off," Aled said.

He'd brought a bag from the car. He fished out a blindfold before shoving the bag into the back of the locker, and Gabriel wondered if Aled had meant for more toys.

"I said strip."

He jumped and hastily stripped. His work clothes were bundled up and shoved into the locker and his dick twitched as Aled locked them away and pocketed the key. If the club was unfamiliar, the lockers weren't. If he failed to please, then he stayed naked until he succeeded. How many mornings had the wardrobes and drawers been locked until he either safeworded or had sex?

He was offered one last chaste kiss before the world was plunged into darkness. For a second, he was all alone on the tiled floor. Then Aled's hands cupped his neck, and the bite struck out of nowhere.

"Fuck!"

His arse was slapped. He whined.

"Swear at me again, and I'll take you downstairs and beat you."

"Y-yes, sir."

"Better. Walk."

He was steered by the shoulders, but made to step back into the lobby first. Immediately, he could feel eyes on him. People were staring. There was an artificial sort of silence and Gabriel couldn't choose between trepidation and arousal. He was naked but for a blindfold and a nipple ring, and everyone was *staring*. But then...he was naked but for a blindfold and a nipple ring, and *everyone* was staring. He felt confident and shy at the same time. He felt grounded and lost at once. Aled's hands were on his shoulders, but there was nothing in front of him. Aled was holding on to him, but not shielding him.

"Stop."

He stopped. The hands vanished. A chair creaked and Aled's hands returned to his hips.

"Kneel."

He sank to the cold floor. The marble was intensely uncomfortable. If he sat forward, it crushed his knees. If he leaned back, it ground against the tops of his feet. But he didn't fidget. He sat perfectly still as Aled raked a hand through his hair, tugging almost painfully at his scalp.

"Open."

He opened his mouth but didn't lean in. Aled was in one of his dangerous moods, and Gabriel was too disoriented by the club to want punishing. Sex in front of staring strangers was enough. Being beaten or humiliated in front of them was — for now — too much.

"Take a deep breath."

The command came after a long pause. Gabriel whimpered, then obeyed. The hand slipped to the back of his neck. He relaxed his throat as the head of a hard cock was pushed past his lips, and tried not to flinch or resist as it carved a hot path past teeth and tongue and throat. It stopped when his nose brushed hair. Behind the blindfold, he closed his eyes and tried to push down the panic. No air. No *air*. *There was no* —

"Hum."

He obeyed on instinct. His lungs ached. The dick in his neck got impossibly bigger. He fisted his hands into the sparse hair of his own thighs. Tears were burning his eyes. *Please, please, please* —

The hand vanished from the back of his neck, but Gabriel stayed perfectly still. He knew the trap. He felt dizzy, but the trap was worse, the trap was worse —

A single finger stroked from his forehead to the crown, then the hand closed and pulled. He reeled in a desperate breath as the wet head came to rest on the tip of his tongue, then closed his lips to hold it in place.

"Very good," Aled murmured. "You've been practising."

Oh, no.

"But it's been six weeks since you deepthroated me, so who've you been practising on?"

Gabriel said nothing.

"You like having other men's dicks in you?"

Nothing.

"You want other men to see you like this?"

Nothing.

The cock slid free. A hand gripped his jaw so hard that Gabriel felt the bruises blossom. He whimpered, and cruel teeth bit his lower lip for the infraction.

"Give them a show, then."

"S-sir?"

"Get up here and fuck yourself until I'm done. Let them all watch those pretty tits of yours. Then when you're done riding it, you can walk over to the bar with my cum running down your legs and get me a coffee. How does that sound?"

It sounded humiliating. It sounded embarrassing. It sounded utterly awful. Everyone would be staring at him the whole time. Then if Aled wanted to lounge around and drink a coffee, he'd fuck Gabriel again after. Two fucks with all these people watching. Two loads to run down his legs. Two rounds of being used like a warm aid to wanking.

It sounded so fucking *good*.

"Thank you, sir."

Chapter Seven

Aled wasn't sure what had inspired him to take Gabriel to the club, but it was an experiment he was definitely going to repeat.

Not only had the jealous stares of other men in the club been one hell of an ego-stroking exercise, but Gabriel had been stoned on submissive bliss. He'd even cosied up in bed that evening for another fuck — but it had been gentle.

And Aled was itching to be…less than gentle.

The next morning was a Saturday. Aled woke up early thanks to a case of morning wood and stole downstairs to check Gabriel's work schedule before sneaking back up and taking his time in carefully stripping Gabriel of his underwear and tying him to the bed. Loose at first — just rough rope looped around each wrist and ankle — then slowly tightening and tightening, ever careful not to wake him, until he was spread-eagled on the bed and immobilised. The blindfold from the night before at the club completed the picture and Aled let himself deliver one gentle kiss to a slack cheek before dragging his power and confidence around himself like a cloak and settling in for the game.

Then he sat back and switched on the TV.

It didn't take long after that. Gabriel wriggled while he slept, and it only took about fifteen minutes of useless squirming to drag him up from the depths. Aled smirked as the sharp gasp ripped into the room, and patted the flat belly shivering by his side.

"Good morning."

"W-what's—what—"

"Demonstrate," Aled interrupted.

There was a sharp pause, then Gabriel snapped his fingers. Left, then right. The safeword for when there was no talking—because Aled had no intention of letting Gabriel's mouth go unused all morning.

"Good."

"Let me go."

"No. Last night was a cute little stage show, but it wasn't good enough. You obviously need to be reminded what a real fuck feels like."

"I did what you told me!"

"I told you to fuck yourself on my cock. You practically made love to it."

"I did it properly!"

"I didn't see blood on my thighs when you were done."

"Oh God, no. No-no-no-no—"

Aled leaned over and gripped Gabriel's jaw in one hand.

"You shut up," he said, "or I'll gag you."

Then he kissed him. Not the reassuring kiss in the car before taking him to the club, but a harsh bite of anger and pain. He ripped at Gabriel's mouth and swallowed the yowl as he shoved his aching dick inside. Gabriel curled into a fuck. He wrapped himself around cock like a glove. But Aled had strapped him down too hard, and it made him tight inside. It was like being milked, and Aled groaned into the begging mouth caught by his own.

Then *fucked*.

He held Gabriel's hips in a bruising grip and pounded into him like a hammer on nails. No aim, no finesse, no skill. A predator taking prey. An aggressor staking a claim. He gave up on the kiss and buried his teeth in Gabriel's neck instead, holding on with his teeth and groaning his lust into the soft, damaged skin while Gabriel—

Screamed. Cried. Begged and pleaded. Dissolved from words to an anguished sobbing that was shoved out of him with every thrust. Then yelled again when Aled came, and called him a bastard when he pulled out, removed the condom and forced the contents into Gabriel's mouth. Cum spilled over swearing lips, but not blood.

Aled smirked. "That was just to take the edge off."

"You fucking—"

Aled slapped him.

"Shut it!" he thundered. "If you can't shut it, I'll make you!"

"Let me go! Let me *go!*"

It was a fight to get the gag in and the strap locked tight, but the screams were soon muffled. Aled sighed in relief. He liked a bit of yelling, but the room was too small for Gabriel to go for his blood-curdling shrieks. The muffled sobbing behind the gag was much better.

"I'll let you out when you earn it," he said. "I was going to fuck your mouth later, but I guess your cunt will have to do. But don't worry. I'll be sure to use protection—can never tell *what* sluts like you are carrying."

The noise Gabriel made was probably casting aspersions on Aled's mother. Gabriel hated condoms. It would make it all the more of a mindfuck if he could really feel his own arousal while Aled supposedly forced him into it.

"What was that?" Aled asked. "You want to suck my dick?"

Gabriel shook his head. Aled caught him by the hair and pulled until he whined.

"I think that was a yes," he crooned. "Maybe we can reach a compromise, hm?"

He straddled Gabriel's lower ribs and began to massage his tits, keeping an ear out for any clicks of the fingers. Aled was bisexual. Tits and pecs, arse or cunt, it was all good as far as he was concerned. His preferences when it came to looks tended to be gender-oblivious things like smiles, shapely bums and freckles. But Gabriel wasn't wired quite the same, and sometimes playing with his boobs and that beautiful nipple ring could catapult him into absolute bliss.

And sometimes it could trigger a dysphoric meltdown and the *R* word.

But while Gabriel squirmed and swore through the gag, his fingers never made a sound as Aled massaged the small pale breasts that cupped his soft cock between them. They were barely more than a handful each, dusted with light fluffy hair after years of HRT, and with beautifully responsive nipples. Gabriel began to cry as Aled teased them into points and twisted the nipple ring until the skin around it swelled and grew painfully hot.

As did his cock.

He didn't titfuck often — not worth the risk, usually — but he took his time and enjoyed it. The slide of soft breasts around his dick, coupled with the faint brushes of hair, was intensely erotic. Aled tipped his head back as he fucked in long, idle strokes. His balls dragged against heaving ribs and stomach. A bead of blood welled up around the nipple ring and stained his fingers. He sucked it off, then slid back down and drove himself back into that used and abused pussy so he could wrap his lips around the bleeding nipple and suck it until the sobbing returned to screams.

"Not quite the blood I was looking for," he said, "but it's a good start."

* * * *

Aled slipped into the bathroom and closed the door with a snap.

It was steamy, the bath full. Gabriel lay stretched out in the water, one arm trailing over the side temptingly. The first aid kit was in pieces all over the sink and counter, and abandoned strips of ropes lay in a pile on the closed toilet lid.

"Hey," Aled whispered, sinking to his knees on the bathmat and propping himself up against the edge. "Bedsheets are changed and dishes are washed. Room for one more?"

Gabriel hummed, and beckoned with a single finger. Aled kissed the side of his head, then stood to strip.

It had been an intense and brutal morning, ended by snapped fingers when the pain of the abused nipple ring had gotten too distracting for Gabriel to enjoy himself anymore. Antiseptic cream, a fresh and slightly smaller ring and a plaster had fixed up the breast and as Aled stepped into the bath behind Gabriel and sank down into the warmth, he felt the hot water and the pliant body that sagged back against his chest fixing his own wounds, too.

"How do you feel?" he whispered, curling his arms around Gabriel's waist and kissing an exposed ear.

"Safe," Gabriel breathed. "Loved. *Tired*."

Aled chuckled. "Me too. And how do I feel?"

"You love me."

Aled tightened his grip a fraction. "I do. Good game?"

"Mhmm."

"Is that a yes?"

"Yeah."

Aled rested his head back against the edge and relaxed. The bath was really too small for this, and he'd not be able to stay long but the simple act helped. The anxious voice in the back of his head fell silent. Gabriel's fingers were stroking a soft pattern into his arm. The water swirled as he turned over, then Aled smiled into the kiss.

"L've you."

"Love you too—*what* are you doing?" Aled asked as a hand curled around his dick. "You'll be so lucky."

"Lucky Lazarri, that's me."

Aled grumbled as he was slowly worked, then closed his eyes and let Gabriel have his way. Once he might have questioned it. Once he might have wondered if it was an apology for the orgasm interrupted by the safeword. But he knew Gabriel better now than those early days and simply let him touch. Only with Gabriel could a hand job be intimate and non-sexual all at once.

When Aled came, it was barely noticeable but for the way Gabriel squeezed gently and kissed his mouth.

"One thing," Gabriel murmured.

"What?"

"Stop using fucking condoms."

Aled laughed. "Hey, you didn't safeword that."

Gabriel grumbled.

"You know the rules."

"Yeah, yeah. Why do you even like them? They feel gross."

"They feel fine," Aled said. "You like ribbed ones."

"Those weren't ribbed."

"Want me to stick to those?"

"If you must," Gabriel muttered. "Rather you didn't use any."

"I know, but I remain unconvinced that your weightlifting shag hasn't got the clap."

"He doesn't! Anyway, he does use them. He thinks if you get cum within a hundred feet of an ovary, you get a baby."

"Oh, bloody Christ," Aled said, and burst out laughing. "Well, at least you can't blame me if you do get pregnant, condoms or no condoms."

"I'd blame Kevin," Gabriel said. "He's the one with a new kid every year."

"Good point," Aled said, then tapped a wet shoulder. "Off. I'm going to get out and get into my pyjamas. Bed, or a cuddle on the sofa with a bad film?"

"I don't mind," Gabriel said. He followed Aled out of the bath and cosied up in the same towel. "You know what I'd like?"

"Oh, here we go."

But the wet, warm body pressed up against his own, and the arms locked around his shoulders like they were about to dance, put paid to any of Aled's protests. He dashed his nose across Gabriel's in a swift, lipless kiss and earned himself a surprised smile.

"Go on," Aled prompted. "What do you want?"

"An orgasm," Gabriel said. "You got four and I only got one and I feel a bit funny downstairs because of it. Like I got all the foreplay then nothing, and I can't scratch the itch. So, will your magic tongue be visiting later?"

Aled grinned. He cupped the back of Gabriel's head. Kissed him until that beautiful body sagged in his arms and the only tension left was in the grip around his neck.

"Sofa," he said. "Put on your favourite film, then open your legs and let me blow your mind."

And his dick, but the mind came first.

Chapter Eight

"Have fun last night, did you?"

Gabriel scowled. Suze was standing on the doorstep wearing an offensively ugly jumper and an even more offensively smug grin.

"Fuck off," he said.

She stuck her shoe in the door before he could close it, then barged her way in and shouted for Aled.

"He's in the shower."

"Taking care of his chafed dick?"

"Not all of us have boyfriends with paper-thin penises," Gabriel said loftily and closed the door. "Want a drink?"

"Yeah, okay."

She followed him into the kitchen and pulled herself up on the counter like a kid as he switched the kettle on. Suze was the same age as Aled but looked closer to Gabriel's age. She was so fair that her skin had almost no sun damage whatsoever from a lifetime spent in the shade and hidden under several layers of factor fifty. Her face was framed by an artificially straight bob of artificially blonde hair. Even her eyes were a pale shade of grey. Her clothes and makeup usually tried to take up the slack, with orange summer dresses, yellow winter jumpers or scarlet lipstick all making regular appearances. She looked like a gaudy twenty-five — until she smiled, which was often, and time revealed itself in pretty crows' feet and cheerful laughter lines.

Gabriel had always found it rather odd that they worked at the same firm, yet bold Suze worked in finance and bland Aled worked in marketing.

"Got plans?" she asked as he fished for teabags.

"Not really. I swapped shifts so I'm not working today."

"Good, you can come with me and Aled."

"He didn't say anything about you two having plans."

"He doesn't know we have them yet."

Gabriel smirked. "I'm good, thanks."

"Come on! I'm taking him suit shopping. Wouldn't you like to see him in a suit?"

"I see him in a suit most days," Gabriel pointed out.

"No, those are his cheap off-the-rail work suits. They're crap. A *proper* suit. *Properly* tailored. It makes a big difference."

"I'll take your word for it," Gabriel said. "I've never done anyone in a proper suit."

Suze rolled her eyes. "He'll look handsome. It's not all about sex."

"What's the point of the suit if it's not going to make him sexier?"

"He'll be handsome!"

"So?"

She huffed and called him shallow, but Gabriel had been called worse. He just shrugged, handed over her tea and headed up the stairs, banging on the bathroom door on the way past and telling Aled that his slapper mate had turned up. The outraged squawk from downstairs made his revenge all the sweeter.

He could see why she'd commented on their sex life when he'd answered the door, though. Aled had left a savage bruise on his neck, probably good enough for Aled's dentist to use as a map. Gabriel rolled his eyes and opened the wardrobe to steal a hoodie or something. He found a black one at the back, and decided to go dark for the day. Jeans. Briefs. Socks, too — why not match? Not like he was going to —

"Coming?"

He jumped violently. Aled chuckled and a damp kiss landed on the back of Gabriel's head.

"Apparently not," Gabriel said as Aled dropped the towel and stepped into a clean pair of boxers.

"Tart. I meant out with me and Suze. Heard her plans from up here."

"Not my thing."

"Not even if I fuck you in a changing room cubicle?"

"Meh. Never appealed to me," Gabriel admitted. "Too many old hangovers about changing rooms in general, I think."

"Fair enough," Aled said, but slid a hand into Gabriel's back pocket and reeled him in regardless. "Come anyway."

"What do I get out of it?"

Teeth bit his ear. His nerves shivered warningly.

"I'm not asking," Aled purred.

"Um. O-okay."

The hand vanished. Gabriel blinked hazily, then swore when he realised he'd agreed.

"That's not fair!"

"Nobody said anything about fair." Aled chuckled, shoving a T-shirt over his head. "Come on. I'm driving because Suze is a bloody maniac and I like being alive. If you're quick, you can kick her out of the front seat."

"I'd rather have a nap in the back," Gabriel groused.

He really wasn't into clothes shopping. More than one guy had tried to take him on a trip — apparently other twinks like that kind of thing — but it had always bored him to tears at best, or reminded him of his mother forcing him into skirts and strappy tops at worst, holding his arm so hard that the bones ached and screaming in his face that he was her daughter, not a fucking dyke. And clothes had never been too much of a turn-on for him. He wasn't into uniforms. He didn't have a thing for heels. Or leather. Or rubber. The nearest he had to an interest in clothes was it was pretty sexy to be naked when the other guy was fully clothed and intending to fuck him without taking anything off. And that was more about the balance of power than whatever the hell anyone was wearing.

So sure, Aled probably would be very sexy in a suit. But it wasn't going to make the trip any more interesting.

"If you come with us, and let me find something good for you, then — "

Aled ducked in again. The hand touched his hip. Lips grazed his ear.

" — I'll call Kevin and we'll arrange something."

Gabriel's breath caught.

We'll arrange something.

Like a kidnap. Like a slave for sale. Like remedial training. Like something scary and violent and so, so good.

"Deal."

He still retreated to the back seat, mainly to text Kevin and think up something for them to do to him. Suze was chatty and cheerful and Gabriel's grouchy mood eased a little when she told stories of Tom's awful overbearing mother and how she'd go spare when she realised Suze had cut her out of the wedding dress proceedings. Because of course that was where they were going first. The big white puffball dress — only it wasn't going to be big, it wasn't going to be white, it wasn't going to be a puffball and Suze wasn't even sure she wanted a dress.

"I need something down the middle," she said. "I look frumpy in a trouser suit. But I don't want to wear a dress. And I'm not entitled to white."

Gabriel sniggered.

"I don't want heels either, but flats just look tatty and grim."

"Go barefoot," Gabriel said. "Sounds like Tom's mum will really hate that."

"Ooh, good shout…"

Gabriel had never been shopping in relation to weddings and had expected them to end up at a bridal shop. To his surprise, they ended up in Leeds city centre and he was towed into a department store rather than a specialist boutique.

Then Suze turned to him and said, "So how do I get an androgynous bride look going?"

"How the hell should I know?" Gabriel asked blankly.

"Well…you know."

"No."

She pinked and gestured vaguely at him. "You must have — you know. Figured out…different clothes."

Gabriel narrowed his eyes. "Why?"

He could feel his hackles rising.

"Because—"

· She must have smelled the danger. She backpedalled hastily and shoved Aled into the menswear section to find suits in a panicked sort of manner. Gabriel stood stock-still and watched them go, jaw working tightly to push down the irritational anger. She hadn't meant anything by it. It was just dumb. Wasn't like her boyfriend hadn't said dumber.

Wasn't like logic did fuck-all for emotions, mind.

It took him a good few minutes and when he cooled to a simmering annoyance instead of a fury, he brought the temperature down even further by wandering over to the fusty old bloke section and picking out some hideous ties for a laugh. By the time he came back to present them to Aled as complementary designs for his best man suit, the irritation had died away.

And he found Suze trying on a waistcoat.

"That's not cut for women," he said automatically.

"But I like it," she argued, doing a little twirl. "Maybe I could wear a suit."

"Thought you didn't want to look frumpy?" Aled interjected.

Gabriel shrugged. "Tight waistcoat—dark colour—over a white blouse, and a white skirt. And if you want to piss off this pompous mother-in-law, wear a pair of gaudy flip-flops."

He'd meant it as a flippant remark, but Suze's face lit up and she went charging off down the escalators to the women's section, leaving them both standing there in bemusement. Gabriel pulled a helpless sort of expression to make Aled laugh, then prodded him into putting back the suit jacket he was holding.

"Pinstripe is ugly."

"I'm heading straight for forty, I'm fat, and I work in marketing. Pinstripe is my area."

Gabriel leaned in. "You also once locked me in my flat for three days and made me buy my way out with sex."

"And I'll do it again if you don't behave."

Gabriel slipped away and found a much nicer solid grey suit. "I am behaving. Look, I'm being helpful. How about this one?"

"When you get helpful, I get suspicious," Aled quipped. "Find me something *I* could get married in. I'm not buying two posh suits."

"What do you need a wedding suit for?" Gabriel asked. "Found someone?"

Technically, their agreement was that both of them could have relationships with other people, but Aled wasn't emotionally wired that way. He did sometimes sleep with other people, usually on his work trips when Gabriel wasn't around for prolonged periods, but he only loved one person at a time.

"Just you."

"You're not marrying me."

"You never know."

Gabriel chuckled. "You'll be waiting a long time for that proposal, sunshine. Here. Go try those one."

He sent him packing into a changing room with a black suit and a grey one, and the collection of ugly ties. He leaned up against the wall to wait, returning to his texts with Kevin.

Me: I'm suit shopping for Aled's mate's wedding.

Kevin: Get one for yours.

Me: Lay off!!

Me: Told you before, we're not getting married.

Me: Although he did drop a hint a minute ago.

Kevin: Told you so.

Kevin: Save some seats at the church for us.

Me: Fuck off!!

Kevin: You mind your language.

Gabriel rolled his eyes but backed out before he could get into trouble. He was rescued from a beating by Suze returning with an armload of clothes and vanishing into the changing rooms. Aled took his time fiddling about with fancy suits, but Suze was quicker. She re-emerged in a matter of minutes in a floaty white blouse, a black women's waistcoat that emphasised her not inconsiderable chest and an ankle-length summer skirt made of white lace, almost see-through. Gabriel snorted when he took in the bright purple flip-flops that finished her off, with a bright white daisy over each big toe.

"Well," he said. "It's a sort-of dress. And it's white."

"Does it look nice?"

"You'll need a proper white skirt underneath. Can see your knickers."

She gave him a smirk and a little wiggle. As she twirled, Gabriel cocked his head.

"Try a short-sleeved blouse," he suggested. "It's still a bit matronly on the top half. Or a V-neck. Showing a bit of cleavage will piss off the mother-in-law too."

"I like the way you think."

She disappeared behind the curtains again, and Gabriel glanced back down at his phone, twirling it around in his hand. Slowly, he pushed off from the wall and went browsing the rails. He'd been planning on just getting something cheap, but—

Well.

Never knew when he might need it again.

Chapter Nine

When Aled had got married, he hadn't made a speech.

Suze had been his best woman. Melissa had had bridesmaids. Dads had stood up to speak. But not Aled. He had said boilerplate vows, laughed and cried through other people's words and never said a thing of his own to all their guests at once, or to his about-to-be-wife in front of their nearest and dearest.

But he would have to speak at Suze's.

And weirdly — despite everything else that needed to go first, and all the time he had to finish it — Aled was struck early on with a sense of urgency about the speech. It was going to be a one-time deal. That much was obvious. And Aled had to pack thirty-odd years of emotion into a single, ten-minute window, for everyone to understand.

Most of all, Suze.

He went looking for photos first, hoping they would jog his memory. The first rainy weekend that rolled around, he got out the ladder and went hunting for the boxes in the attic. They were still labelled in Melissa's neat hand from their last big house move, and — because his wife had been infinitely more organised than Aled — it was easy to find the family albums that he'd inherited from Dad. He took the boxes downstairs to spread them out and decided to lose himself in his own history as the rain hammered on the conservatory roof.

And it was easy to do. Dad had been snap-happy. He had Aled's baby pictures, even though Aled hadn't been adopted until he was a little kid. The earliest picture that Aled could find of Suze was — ironically — their wedding photo. Him in his Spider-Man T-shirt with his hair sticking up all over the place, her in a lacy veil made out of Nana's curtains and beaming toothily around the wedding cake Mum had made for them.

"That's cute," Gabriel said.

Aled had spread out the photos on the coffee table, making notes for his best man's speech and the greatest opportunity he'd ever have to get revenge on all the things Suze had ever done to annoy him. He'd started when he got home from work and Gabriel had flopped down on the sofa behind him with a bowl of homemade soup once he'd returned from the gym.

"Did you marry your best mate in nursery school?"

"Didn't go to nursery school," Gabriel said. "Mum only made us go to school to stop the social turning up at the door. But I gave a bunch of daisies to Jenny Simpson when we were seven. We dated for a whole week. That's pretty much marriage for me, right?"

Aled grinned.

"I wasn't allowed to play with Jenny anymore once my mother found out."

"Why?"

"Jenny was black," Gabriel said simply and Aled grimaced.

"Your mother just gets better and better."

"Tell me about it," Gabriel muttered. "Why are you giving Suze away, then? What happened to her dad?"

"Probably back in prison," Aled said. "He's been in and out of jail longer than Suze has been alive."

"Oh, Christ."

"I don't think Suze has even seen him since she was about thirteen. Her brother's the same way."

"What about her mum?"

"Not right in the head," Aled said. "I don't know if she was ill before she met Suze's dad or not, but he certainly didn't help matters. I don't know if she'll come. Suze has invited her, but...yeah, I doubt she'll show up."

"So you're pretty much the only family going?"

"Probably."

"That's sad," Gabriel said wistfully.

Aled shrugged. "It is what it is. There were a lot of problem families round where we grew up. Suze wasn't the only one."

"I grew up in a tower block in Hackney," Gabriel said. "Seven of us in one flat. She used to lock us out during the day, too. No prizes for guessing what my mum did for a living."

"On the game?"

"Bingo."

"Is that why you're touchy about being paid for it?" Aled asked curiously. It had always struck him as a little odd. Nothing got Gabriel angrier than when a hookup left money like he was a prostitute. They could play pretend sometimes, but Aled had rapidly learned not to spring the idea on him out of nowhere. He'd go nuclear if he got the impression he was actually being paid for it, and Aled had always thought it odd for someone who was so sex-positive.

"Probably." Gabriel shrugged. "I got out, though."

Aled leaned his head back to rest them on Gabriel's knees. The sofa creaked, and a kiss landed the wrong way up on his forehead.

"Didn't think I'd ever make a nice house, a proper job and a steady boyfriend."

Aled smirked, then said, "Me neither, actually."

"Why? Wasn't your mum a doctor?"

"Yeah, but I wasn't that smart. And I was violently kinky. I figured that out pretty young, really, and I figured I'd end up in prison for something awful like Suze's dad," Aled said. "I had a good few years being fucked up about it. Without Suze, I wouldn't have made it out."

He leafed through the pictures until he found one of their teenage years. Both in the ugly green uniform, him looking like a Christmas tree thanks to the combination of a bottle-green jumper and bright red hair. Suze with her natural brown and a mouth full of braces. And Melissa, too, with her fiery red mane and beautifully superior expression.

"Jesus," Aled muttered. "Look how fucking *young* we were."

Gabriel leaned over his shoulder to look and laughed. "Oh my God. What are you, twelve?"

"Fourteen."

"I was barely at school yet."

"*Thanks*," Aled drawled and dropped the picture again. He shifted up the pad on his knee and wrote a couple of words.

"What's that?"

"Going to be my speech."

"You going for funny or sentimental?"

"Ideally both," Aled said. "And embarrassing. Can't forget embarrassing."

"Oh, of course not."

Gabriel switched on the TV after a while and let Aled work in peace, but the truth was that Aled wasn't sure what to write. Suze was essentially his sister. He had a lifetime of ammunition. Over thirty years of things to say — and it meant that he didn't know *what* to say. Did he tell the story of their pseudo-wedding when they were little kids? Did he tell them about Suze daring him to ride his bike over the lock at Canal Lane and Dad going mad when he inevitably fell off and broke his arm? Did he tell about the time she didn't know how to dump her boyfriend in sixth form, so snogged Aled outside their English class to make the boyfriend dump her instead? Did he tell of the day she nearly burned the flat down, their first year in university, because she hadn't figured out that pasta was boiled in water and not pan-fried at two in the morning when drunk?

Did he say Tom was mad for marrying her, or that he was the luckiest man in the world?

Did he say what she meant to him, or leave it lying in the spaces between them, where they both knew full well what the other meant?

Did he disturb a lifetime of never *needing* to say it?

Suze is my best friend.

The words appeared under his hand like magic. He felt as though he was watching someone else write them as they began to flow, and sat back to see what came out.

She is my sister, my friend, my confidante, my cheerleader, my coach and my rock. We grew up together. I don't have a biological sister, but Suze was as good as. She has been there for almost my entire life and is woven into every aspect of it. She knows everything there is to know about me and, unfortunately for her, I can say the same. So what can I say about her in front of an audience? What can I share in front of all the important people in her life that won't result in my death by the end of the evening?

He didn't pause.

I could tell you about the fact that I married her first. We were best friends from the day we met, and we married not long afterwards. I wore my best Spider-Man shirt. She wore her brightest wellies. She punched me for trying to take the first slice of cake and wore my Haribo ring for a whole week before eating it. And she was sick for a whole day afterwards, which she richly deserved for eating my wedding ring in the first place.

Over his shoulder, Gabriel chuckled. Aled smiled but kept going.

I could tell you about her first proper boyfriend. He was terribly interesting, because we were thirteen and he had a real tattoo that his older brother had given him. He smoked, too – it took a while before we all figured out they were just menthol cigarettes, but nobody said we were smart at our school. But Ryan decided that he didn't like Suze having a male best friend who lived five doors down and had seen her in her training bra more than he had. Suze decided she didn't like his arm after that and broke it in two places. Understandably, they split up. That was Suze's first foray into the world of romance.

"Seriously?"

I could tell you about the day I met my future wife, when Suze shoved me out onto the playing fields and said if I didn't go and introduce myself to the girl I'd been staring at for weeks, then she'd burn my entire comic collection. She used the exact same threat when I was dithering about whether to propose to the same girl, years later. It was just as effective.

"Nerd."

"Shut up," Aled said, ears heating.

"It's okay. Nerds make great sex gods."

Aled snorted.

I could tell you about the day she met Tom, when she texted me that some spotty git at the student cafe had asked her out and asked if I'd set her up. I told her that I hadn't, but given she had a shit taste in men, the fact she didn't like this one probably meant he was her future husband, so she'd better say yes.

"Suze had a shit taste in men?"

"Before Tom," Aled murmured as he wrote. "Every single one of them was a controlling prick. At best. At worst, a couple of them were downright abusive. Talking to her never worked, so I used to provoke them into slagging me off in front of her, because that usually did. I even tried to pick a fight with one of them and he completely destroyed me, but it worked."

"Define destroyed you," Gabriel said.

"Put me in the hospital with three cracked ribs."

I could tell you about the day she texted me, maybe six months later, and admitted she'd run into the spotty git again and there was something about his smile. I said he must have turned into a shitbag since asking her out the first time, so to avoid him. Naturally, she didn't listen to me.

Gabriel turned the TV down and leaned over Aled's shoulder, looping both arms around his neck to watch the words unfold.

I could tell you about the day she turned to me in a third-year lecture and said, "I think I'm in love with Tom. And it doesn't feel like the last time." That's the day I saw today coming. That's the day I thought, "This is serious." That's the day I realised that my best friend had fallen in love and I wasn't going to be the only man in her life who was good for her anymore.

"Does that sound too arrogant?"

"Read it all through when you're done and see."

"Okay."

And that was one of the happiest days of my life, ladies and gentlemen. Because I have loved Suze since the day I met her. She is one of the most important people in my life and to see her finally fall in love with a man who deserved it, who deserved her, *was the most incredible privilege.*

He paused. The pen hovered. Then —

Suze is and always has been a force of nature. She is beautiful — never more so than today — and she is clever. She is unstoppable. She is the sun in a sometimes dark and lonely world. She is nothing short of glorious. And I could stand here and tell you stories until the sun sets, but the one I actually want to tell you is this one.

Gabriel squeezed lightly.

Once upon a time, there was a girl who met a boy. The girl was one of the most brilliant women ever made. And the boy knew that. He took one look at her and knew. He looked at her like she was going to achieve her dreams, with or without him. He looked at her like she was beautiful, from when she was dressed to kill to when she rolled out of bed at two in the afternoon with her makeup halfway to her knees. He looked at her like she was everything he ever wanted, even when it had been so long that the girl was a woman, and the boy was a man. He looked at her like he was meeting her for the first time, over and over again, and never was it clearer than today.

The pen was shivering faintly in his fingers.

I gave my sister away today, and even if that phrase were literal and this was the last time we spoke, I would do it all again. Because today I gave my best friend's hand to the man who has worshipped the ground she's walked on for all these years. I watched her marry a man who knows how lucky he is to have her, who has never been ashamed to say he loves her, who has never shied from challenging her when she needed it, and never failed to step up and support her when she wanted him to. There aren't many men who deserve a wife like Suze, but Tom is one of those men.

Lips touched his ear lightly, and their warmth pierced him right through to the middle.

This has been one of the proudest and happiest days of my life, and I would invite you all to join me in a toast to Thomas and Suzanne Hooper.

Gabriel reached out and toppled the pen from Aled's grip with a single finger before locking both arms back around his neck and squeezing tight.

"You old romantic," he murmured.

"Yeah, well."

"Why don't you write me love notes like that, hm?"

"Marry me and I might."

"It's not *that* good," Gabriel said with a laugh.

"Anyway, you squirm and get embarrassed when I say something nice to you."

"That's why you write it down and leave it somewhere for me to find where nobody's watching," Gabriel teased, then pushed himself up off the sofa. "Want anything from the kitchen?"

"Nah."

"Okay. Going for a shower."

"Good, you're humming a bit."

"Hey!"

Aled flashed a grin over his shoulder, then turned the page on the notebook as he heard Gabriel go upstairs.

Dear Gabriel.

Well, why not?

C h a p t e r   T e n

Gabriel stepped down off the train and fished in his pocket for his phone.

Me: At the station :)

He sent it to both Aled and Chris, then pulled himself up on the fence to wait. He'd been waiting for their Lake District adventure to arrive for ages, so he could wait just a little bit longer. And from the text Chris had sent from Manchester Piccadilly, Gabriel guessed he'd be on the next one coming. Not like there were many trains coming up into the darkest depths of the Lake District at this time in the evening.

Chris: 10 minutes

Aled: Chris there yet?

Gabriel grinned. He'd bent Aled's ear for hours about the trip before he'd left. All the new trails they were going to explore, all the planning Chris had done, all the excitement. And not about cycling. This felt...date-like, but not a date. It felt like a relationship. It felt like...

Like that moment when things slid from being forced and awkward and still figuring out whether they wanted each other, to a natural kind of company.

And he knew that Aled could sense it. And unlike all his stupid fears and jittery weirdness when Aled had first asked him to move in, Gabriel knew something else too.

He knew that Aled was pleased for him.

Me: Ten minutes.

Aled: Check the front pocket of your backpack.

Gabriel raised his eyebrows and shifted the pack off. The front pocket was usually empty, or reserved for rubbish out on hikes, but when he unzipped it, there was a note folded up inside, his name neatly printed on the outside.

"What the—"

Dear Gabriel,
You wanted an old romantic love note, so here it is —
Whenever you go away, you come back lit up like the surface of the sun, almost too brilliant to touch. You come back so glorious that it's plain to see you could be anywhere, have anyone, do anything and yet every time you come back to me. You arrive talking a mile a minute about what you've done, the things you've seen, the way you feel and it's the most beautiful thing I've ever seen because you're brimming over with the need to share those things with me and the desire to mix your life with mine.

There's days I still look at you like you're brand new, and I can't believe I've navigated the turbulent waters to get to you. I know why we started, and I know why I'm still here, but there's moments where you tip your head back on the sofa and smile, or you put your feet in my lap while you're reading, or you invade the bathroom to sit on the edge of the bath and talk to me and I can't fathom how I collected enough luck in a lifetime to keep you near.

And yet even as I wonder how, I never wonder why. I don't know how I made you love me, but I know that you do. I can see it in the way you kiss me on sunny mornings, the way you smile at me when I pick you up from work, the way you turn into me in the night and wrap yourself around me, the way you wind me up with that little smirk on your face. I've no idea how I made you fall in love with me, but I have no doubt that it happened.

You are my world. Others may visit my world now then, perhaps even stay a while and set up their own homes in your heart. But I know I'm there, and that's all I ever needed.

You wanted an old romantic love note, so there it was.

Aled x

Gabriel bit his lip, swallowing against a little lump in his throat. Oh, man. Christ, how did he get so lucky? A partner who loved him for who he was, and partly because of his polyamorous nature instead of in spite of it, and a new boyfriend who was sweet and fun and —

And a *boyfriend*.

Aled felt more like a partner than anything else. It felt oddly juvenile to stick the word boyfriend onto the relationship he had with Aled. He was older, more sombre, had a dangerous edge over that fuzzy centre. Chris was — younger, clumsier, still a little bit rough around the edges like Gabriel. He wasn't so sure of himself. And it was fun and familiar territory, to both be out of their depth but kind of enjoying figuring out how to swim together.

And Aled loved to watch him do it.

Gabriel clutched the letter close like a lovesick moron for a second, before folding it up carefully and putting it away in his wallet as the next train rattled into the station. It was almost empty, the windows glowing empty in the twilight, and Gabriel held up his arms to the only man who clattered off it, bag on his back and bike handles between his hands.

"Hello," Chris said.

"C'mere."

The kiss was sharp and hard and crackling with brilliance, and Chris looked a little dazed as they parted again.

"Um," he said. "Hello."

"You said that," Gabriel remarked, then laughed. "Come on. Let's find this B&B."

"What's got into you?"

"Just—good day. Good day." He patted the wallet in his pocket and allowed himself a secret smile. "Come on, let's go. I'm not sleeping out here."

It was cold and dark, but Chris had a knack for finding the good places. The B&B was only a short bike ride away and it glowed out of the gloom like a warm fire. They were treated to a hot dinner, the lady running the place clearly taking them for a cute straight couple and twittering about when she was young and her husband still romantic, then they were shown up to a room in the eaves of the converted cottage, with a pristine if tiny ensuite tucked away in the corner and left to their own devices.

Ordinarily, sex.

But —

"D'you mind sharing?" Chris asked awkwardly.

Gabriel almost laughed. The bed was — of course — a double, and it wasn't like they hadn't slept together before. In both senses of the word. But the awkward flush on Chris' cheeks waylaid it and he cocked his head, the good mood bubbling up into a contented patience.

"Did you not book a double?"

"Twin."

"Well, I'm game if you are," Gabriel said and leaned forward to peck his cheek. "I'm going for a shower."

He mulled it over under the hot water. He and Chris had only had sex a couple of times, and Chris didn't seem to like much in the way of foreplay or even interaction. Was Chris asexual? It would make a bit of sense, really, but then, he could also just have some specialist kink. Gabriel had slept with more than one guy who liked an extremely passive partner, and it wasn't like the stick-it-in-and-shoot-off method did nothing for Gabriel.

Mind made up, he stepped out and dried off before dropping the towel back over the rail and walking out naked. Chris, sitting on the edge of the bed scrolling through his Instagram feed, instantly averted his eyes and Gabriel climbed up on the bed behind him and looped his arms over his shoulders.

"It's up to you," he said softly, "but I kind of like the idea of you sleeping with me when I'm *really* asleep, if you know what I mean."

Chris coughed. "Um. Like —"

"Like if you want to do something in the night, then just do it," Gabriel said and kissed his ear. "Consider it standing consent for the whole night."

He'd wanted to do it for a long time, but it would be a huge trigger for Aled to even attempt it and Kevin's baseball bat of a cock would wake him up before they got anywhere near the actual sex part. Part of Gabriel thought Chris wouldn't go for it, but a larger part of him *wanted* Chris to go for it.

If he liked unresponsive sex, that was.

"Up to you," he whispered then kissed his jaw and let go. "I'm going to sleep."

Chris coughed. "Okay." His voice was a rasp and the contours of his trousers weren't quite the same as usual.

Gabriel smirked, but hid it under the covers.

* * * *

There was a pressure all along his spine. And inside him. He was—wet? Something was—

Gabriel blinked muzzily and relaxed again. Chris. Chris was lying on his back, fucking into him in deep, rhythmic strokes. One hand was toying with his nipple ring. He didn't know where the other one was. Chris' entire weight was on him, the thrusts more idle rolls of the hips. The sparks of pain and pleasure from it roused Gabriel a little, and he stroked a hand down to his cock. What if he jerked off while Chris was inside? What if—

The groan in his ear and sudden shudder in Chris' rhythm said he'd woken up too late.

For a second, the weight increased. Then Chris pulled out, and the mattress bounced. He was gone. The ensuite door closed and Gabriel rolled onto his back and spread his legs to continue playing with himself. He must have slept like the dead. He was wide open and dripping and none of it was Chris'. He must have gloved up again. Gabriel fingered some of it out and soothed his throbbing cock with it then began to jerk it harder to the thought of what had just happened.

He'd been turned over and fucked into like a sex toy. Like a breathing sex doll. What if Chris kept him for just that purpose, like one of Aled's slave games, but long term? And not a game? They could date and they could have fun and they could be all normal on the outside, then Chris would just roll him over in bed and shove it in him without a care. That was all Gabriel was. A toy, a hole, a —

Climax hit him like a freight train. He gasped breathlessly as sense swept away in a wildfire, then sagged bonelessly into the bed when the tsunami receded into a gentle, pleasurable tide.

"Fuck," he whispered. "God*damn*."

He was definitely doing that again.

Once his heartbeat had returned to normal, he slipped out of bed and found a pair of boxers from his overnight bag. He tapped on the bathroom door lightly and tried the handle, before slipping inside — and hesitating.

"Chris?"

Chris was standing at the sink, simply staring at himself in the mirror. Gabriel approached hesitantly and smoothed his fingers over tense shoulders.

"Did you — did you not like that?"

Chris' jaw tightened.

"Yes."

"So…"

There was a long silence.

"It's okay if you liked it," Gabriel prompted gently. "I did."

"Did you?"

"Yes."

"Why? You didn't even get off."

"Finished myself off," Gabriel quipped. "And it's not all about the orgasm. I like the feeling of someone in me, whether I get off or not."

Chris grunted.

"What's wrong?"

He shrugged. "I don't know. I'm just a bit...I don't know. Confused."

"Well, you liked it and I like—"

"Does Aled do that with you?"

Gabriel slid his arms around Chris' waist and leaned into his back.

"No," he said. "Aled's got violent kinks, and it upsets him sometimes. So he doesn't like doing anything where consent gets a bit questionable."

"But does he—"

There was a pause.

"Does he just hold you down and—and do you? Sometimes?"

"Pretty often, yeah."

"And you don't—say anything, or move or...?"

Gabriel quirked his lips. "Sometimes I can't. Gags, handcuffs, rope—it's not always just him, me and the nearest mattress."

Things were starting to come together in Gabriel's head a little.

"Do you like that? When I don't move or make a sound?"

The tension rippled up Chris' back, and Gabriel squeezed.

"It's fine if you do."

"Is it?"

"Yes."

"I'm not so sure."

"I am," Gabriel said simply. "Aled likes to hurt me. Nothing wrong with it, because he has my permission to do it. Same with you. If you like me to just…I don't know, just lie there, or not be aware you're doing it, then that's okay too. Because you had my permission."

He had the vaguest sense that there was something else lurking around the edges of Chris' mind, and it wasn't as simple as he was making it out to be, but the tension eased a little and Gabriel kissed the centre of his back where the spine passed the shoulder blades. He couldn't push it if Chris was still airing ideas. The final conclusion might not be anything like the early thoughts. Gabriel had slept with enough experimenters and done enough experimenting of his own to know that.

"What's the weirdest thing you've ever done?" Chris whispered.

"Eh?"

"Sexually."

"We-ell. I didn't do it. Does it count if I refused to do it?"

"Yeah."

"This one guy used to suck on my tits like he was trying to drink from me. I didn't mind that bit, but I drew the line when he wanted to get me pregnant so he could do it for real."

Chris' back stiffened again — but then shivered as he started to laugh.

"Seriously?"

"On my life," Gabriel said solemnly. "He was so keen on the idea. Even said he didn't mind if I got it aborted, as long as I'd started to produce the goods. He said if he kept drinking from me then I'd not stop lactating, so I didn't need to actually *have* a baby. He offered to pay for somewhere for me to live near to where he worked and everything, like a proper sugar daddy deal, just so he could drop by and get breakfast off me every morning before work."

"Oh my God—"

"Oh no, you want the best parts?"

Chris raised his eyebrows.

"He was married to a much younger woman and had two kids with her, but his wife thought it was weird and wouldn't let him suck on hers. And the icing on the cake?"

"I'm scared of the icing."

"I later ended up going out with his nephew and found out he was a reverend."

"*Ew!*"

Chris finally turned around at that. He hung on, banging his face into the side of Gabriel's and laughing like a drain. His soft cock rubbed up against Gabriel's thigh and Gabriel wondered what its deal really was, before shoving the whole thing out of his mind.

"Come on," he said. "I need a shower and not to be thinking about the good reverend and his breastfeeding fetish. Then do you want to head out early and hit up the first trail?"

"Sounds good."

His arm was caught before he could step into the shower cubicle and a swift kiss dashed against his chin.

"Sorry for being weird."

"It's okay," Gabriel said, and kissed back. Properly. On the mouth. "I like weird."

"Just not…breastfeeding reverends weird."

"Yeah, no, not *that* weird."

Chris slipped out after that and left Gabriel to his shower. And as Gabriel tipped his head back under the spray, he smiled at the showerhead.

A partner who wrote him love letters. The boyfriend who was still figuring himself out. And there he was in the middle, happy with the both of them for entirely different reasons. So there was something going on in Chris' head that he wasn't privy to yet, so what? Gabriel was sure he'd come out of his shell eventually, and whatever it was couldn't be all that strange, after all.

At least, he hoped not.

Because this right here was perfect, and he didn't want a single thing to change.

Chapter Eleven

Gabriel: Treat me like a whore when I get home.

Aled raised his eyebrows and pushed back from the desk. Thank God for having his own office. Casually, he strolled to the door and closed it before sinking back down and picking up the phone. He couldn't quite draw the blinds on the windows that surrounded him on all sides, but he could at least lock down the sound.

"Hello?"

"It's me," he drawled, in his best don't-you-know-who-I-am voice.

"Oh! Hi."

"Care to explain yourself?"

Gabriel had been away in the Lake District with Chris since Monday and the only updates Aled had had were a couple of hillside selfies and a photo of his train ticket home with a couple of love hearts and a begging letter to be collected from Leeds train station. They were all he usually got. They were all he was expecting.

Not text messages about being a whore.

"I'm all pent-up. I need some release."

"Chris not up to it?"

"He doesn't like to play like you do."

Gabriel sounded breathless. And echoing. Aled smirked. He'd been wanking in a bathroom.

"Are you in a public toilet?"

"Um. Yes."

"You're in some tin can on a hiking trail, aren't you?"

"Yeah."

"You jerked off?"

"Y-yeah—"

Aled dropped the silky tone and sat forward to prop his elbows on the desk and poke his emails, play-acting the boredom as though Gabriel could see straight through the phone.

"Well, sounds like you have the whore act down. What d'you need me for?"

"Are you kidding?" Gabriel hissed. "Who's never wanked in a toilet? Come on! I need more than—than—"

"That being so fucking desperate you dropped your pants in a dirty bog and fucked your own fingers, moaning like a bitch in heat?" Aled returned.

Gabriel caught his breath.

"Yeah. Definitely a whore."

"P-please."

"Knock it off with your please. Plenty of men in the Lake District would like a go at you if you want to act like a whore."

"Don't want them," Gabriel whispered. "I want *you*."

That was more like it. Aled bit back on a wide grin. He drummed his fingers on the desk. "Uh-huh. And what exactly does 'treat me like a whore' mean?" he asked. "That doesn't exactly close off many options with you."

He sat back in his chair as he spoke. When his secretary knocked on the window of his fishbowl of an office and held up a sheaf of papers that needed signing, he simply assumed a pleasant smile and mimed shooting himself in the head, then held up five fingers like he was on a boring old conference call.

"I don't know. Beat me. Fist me. Something that really hurts and makes me come apart at the seams."

"You're going to have to be more specific," Aled drawled.

"Fist me," Gabriel said breathlessly. "And make it hurt. *Really* hurt. Like—like no preparation and open your hand inside and everything. Then when you're fistfucking me, make me come. But like—like so I come, but I feel bad for doing it—"

Aled chuckled. That was easy. Get buried to the wrist, then refuse to leave until Gabriel jerked himself off. There was no way he could get that much inside with absolutely no preparation, not without causing serious damage beyond the limits of any kink either of them had, but he could minimise it. Usually he used enough lube to grease a battleship when fisting and went about it like he wanted to set a record for the longest game ever played. But he could always scrimp on the oil and save a little time for other activities. Leave a good sting behind. And the longer he was there, the more it would hurt.

"All right," he said. "But let's make something very clear. You asked for this. Literally asked. So one moan, one complaint, one protest, and I'll cut you. Every time you pretend like you don't love every second, I'll cut you again. And I'll use whatever I like to do it."

Gabriel sucked in a breath. Aled waited, the dangerous edge dissolving for a moment. He liked bloodplay. And Gabriel didn't.

"Colour?" Aled prompted softly when the silence echoed for too long.

It echoed a little longer before Gabriel answered.

"Yellow."

"Talk to me," Aled murmured.

Another pause.

Then— "No knives."

"No knives," Aled agreed. "Anything else?"

"No."

"Colour?"

"Green."

He could say more. Reassure. Coax. Talk about it.

But Gabriel was still in the Lake District and was fucking himself in a grubby outhouse next to a random cafe because he wanted something wilder than Chris was prepared to give him. And it increasingly felt like Chris was becoming a part of Gabriel's life, and—by default—part of Aled's.

There'd be plenty of words—some other time.

Aled leaned forward, slammed the phone down in its cradle, then picked it up again and pressed a familiar five digits.

"Hi, Sarah. Sorry about that, had Adams bending my ear about the budget. Pop back through and I'll slap a signature on 'em."

* * * *

Aled looped the belt over the coat hanger and shut the wardrobe door before turning back to the bed.

Gabriel was spread-eagled on a layer of bloodstained towels. His back was slick with sweat. His cunt gaped from the damage Aled's fist had done to it. His arse resembled hamburger meat—raw, pink and still bleeding. He was shivering faintly, eyes closed and fists screwed up in the pillows. Aled hadn't bothered to tie him down. He'd been so eager for the pain that they'd had to stop for a spit-fuck on the way home from the train station and Aled hadn't needed to so much as threaten to get the rope out to keep him in place.

Carefully, he braced his weight with his hands either side of Gabriel's ribs and leaned down to press a gentle kiss behind one exposed ear.

"Game over."

The long, shuddering breath was more like a sob.

"Cry," Aled whispered.

The sobs racked his slim frame and Aled let it. He was no stranger to the emotional fallout of an intense scene. He simply waited it out, stroking that unblemished back until they eased, then kissing Gabriel's ear once more.

"Stay right there for me, sweetheart, and let me get the first aid kit."

"Okay."

The kit was in the top drawer as always but Aled nipped to the linen closet for fresh towels. They were warm from the pipes that ran up the back of the cupboard, and he draped one over Gabriel's back like a blanket before popping the lid on the kit and getting out the wipes and antiseptic cream.

"Need to hold my hand?"

"Yes, please."

The grip was tight and pained as Aled removed the blood from where he'd beaten Gabriel seventeen times with the taped-shut belt buckle for complaining about the fistfucking. Technically, he had owed twenty-one lashes, but he'd sensed a red coming from the grey tinge and gritted teeth by the time he'd reached seventeen. It wasn't like Gabriel would have been in any state to count.

"Okay?" he murmured as he started to smooth the antiseptic cream over the wounds.

"Mm."

"How do you feel?"

"Safe. Looked after."

"How do I feel?"

"You love me."

Aled squeezed his hand gently.

"What brought that on?" he murmured as he worked, and Gabriel sighed.

"Just—I needed to come like my brain was going to get ripped out of my head," he croaked. "Chris fucked me once, but it was like foreplay almost. I was all pent-up."

"I could tell," Aled chuckled. "Still sex-shy, is he?"

"Yeah."

"If you needed heavy violence, why didn't you call Kevin?"

"He's still in Spain with Judith and the kids."

"Ah," Aled said.

"Not—not too bad for you?"

"No. About the limit, but not over," Aled said.

"G'd."

The blood had clotted neatly. Aled wiped his hands off on a spare hand towel then folded up the duvet to cover Gabriel's legs. He was still looking faintly grey, so Aled made him promise to stay there before heading downstairs to make a cup of sweet tea.

It *had* been about at Aled's limit. He got off on violence in a big way, but there was only so far he could indulge it. He preferred mind games to an outright beating, using sex as a weapon rather than just a plain old weapon, and the beating had driven him to his own edge. He made a cup for himself as well as Gabriel and took a packet of biscuits back up with him on the side of the tray.

Gabriel had turned on his side and turned the towels into the wrap for a human burrito. Aled coaxed the tea down him then slid down to lie on the bed with him and lifted his arm. The speed with which Gabriel slid into his hold and the easy weight that relaxed against his chest made the knot in Aled's stomach release.

"Okay?" Gabriel whispered.

"Yep." Aled squeezed gently. "Tell me again?"

"I feel safe."

"Good."

"You love me."

"I do."

An arm was wound out of the towels and locked over Aled's chest. A little kiss found the edge of his neck.

"How far off was the red?" Aled asked.

"About two more."

"Okay."

"Why?"

"I knew you were heading for it. Wanted to make sure you would —"

"You know I would have."

"Yeah. Just my brain being daft."

"Shut up, brain."

Aled laughed as his sternum was rapped by hard knuckles. He caught them, kissed them and tucked them under his chin.

"The fisting was *great*," Gabriel murmured sleepily.

"Yeah?"

"Mhmm. It's so fucking hot when you wiggle your fingers inside me."

"Weirdo."

"Fuck off."

Aled laughed.

"I like it," Gabriel breathed. "An' you're not so big as Kevin. Kevin's fists are like—like they're good, but he rips his hand out like that too and it's too wide. Like he's gonna rip my tubes out too."

Aled winced. "Thanks for that imagery."

"S'true."

"So I have nicer hands?"

"For fisting."

"I'll take it," Aled said. "Not too sure I want to be in that deep when you come again, mind."

"Why?"

"I thought you were going to break my thumb."

He felt Gabriel's smirk against his neck. The truth was, it was usually hot as hell. Gabriel had incredibly powerful orgasms. If Aled watched carefully, he could sometimes *see* the uterine contractions through the planes of his stomach. Gabriel didn't want a hysterectomy in case it made them less intense, and Aled couldn't blame him. Having any part of him inside when Gabriel went off was like having his own climax ripped out of him, whether it was around his cock or his hand.

Plus, it was pretty difficult to fake it, so Aled always knew if he was on the right track with a new game.

"How was the Lake District, apart from sexually frustrating?"

"Good. We should go sometime. Lots of cabins in the middle of nowhere."

"Oh aye?"

"Mm. And tall hedges to hide behind. And woods. And—"

"I get the idea. Lots of places to bend you over in the open air."

"Yup."

"Chris not into that either?"

"Nope."

"Shame."

"Yeah, but it was fun," Gabriel said. "I like him. He's good company. He's sweet. And he cuddles *lovely*."

"That's not a sentence."

"Whatever."

"So what you need is a nice break with Chris, all romantic and sporty and nice cuddles, then along comes the monster in the night..."

Gabriel tensed up beside him. "Oh my God. What happens?"

"You heard a noise. Leave him sleeping. Go to look — because why not? Nothing dangerous in the Lake District. It'll be an owl or a fox. Something cute and harmless. So you open the cabin door in the dark—"

Gabriel curled up tight against his side.

"He forces his way in. Gets a hand around your mouth and tells you to be quiet. If you shut up and do as you're told, nobody gets hurt. If you don't, everybody dies. No witnesses, see. Nobody will believe you if nobody hears anything, but he won't have any witnesses screwing things up for him."

Gabriel whimpered.

"He takes you out on the porch and tells you to strip. He likes your piercing. Sits you on his lap and plays with it while he fingers you. He plays you like a lover, and that's why it goes wrong. Because you come. Sluts like you always come. And when you're done gushing over him like a burst water main, he smiles and whispers to you. Do you know what he says?"

"N-no—"

"He says, 'Now you owe me one.'"

Despite the entire evening, Gabriel was wanking to Aled's words. Aled smirked but made no move to take part.

"He sits there and makes you treat him like a lover. Kiss him, touch him, act like you want to be there. And that's the biggest betrayal, because the more you work to get him aroused, the more you like it. By the time you start riding his cock, you're gagging for it. You come again without even touching yourself, and you're begging for his cum before your climax is even over."

Gabriel groaned deeply in his ear. He was getting closer. Higher. *Closer.*

"But he shoves you off," Aled breathed, "and comes on your face and tits instead of inside you. And when you're wiping it off with your fingers and sucking them clean, he grabs you by the hair and whispers in your ear—"

He reached down. Leaned over. Brushed a kiss to Gabriel's ear just as he touched the hot desperation rutting against his thigh.

"'Same time tomorrow, slut.'"

Gabriel came with a shuddering gasp, and Aled caught the sound in his mouth. The orgasm shook the whole bed, then rattled away into the dusk like it had never been. A damp hand slid up Aled's belly. A breathless mouth sucked a kiss into place over his nipple. Aled stroked back damp hair and smiled against Gabriel's hairline.

"Nice idea?"

"Please. *Please*."

"Well, maybe when your Chris isn't so wound up and you're not bleeding from the arse."

"Whenever. Sooner. Just steal me. *Please*."

Aled chuckled and kissed his neck.

"Maybe I'll talk to Kevin sometime. See if we can't work out a joint family holiday away, the whole lot of us."

He filed it away and turned on his neck to fold Gabriel up into a boneless kind of hug. There was plenty of time for new games and new boundaries. Aled wasn't worried about them right now, or indeed anything at all.

However things with Chris played out, it wouldn't change these moments here, in the quiet serenity of their room.

Chapter Twelve

"No way," Gabriel said.

It was Saturday. He had another dominant to see. A great lunch to enjoy. Holiday photos to make fun of. Maybe a trip to a workshop to be put in his place after such a long break from the man who could kill him without even trying, and who had—bar Aled—the greatest grip on his life.

And more to the point, he didn't give a flying fuck about—

"They're *flowers*, Gabriel. I don't want to go pick flowers."

"*I'm* not the best man."

It turned out that middle-aged marketing types could pout. Gabriel snickered at the beseeching look but wasn't swayed

"I don't do weddings and I certainly don't do wedding flowers," he said. "Anyway, I've got plans. Judith's making her carbonara and I'm not missing out on that again."

"Going to play?"

"Nah, just going for a catch-up. I haven't seen them since before they went on holiday, and Kevin had that job in Huddersfield for a fortnight. It's been too long and your best man duties are not trumping a visit to their house." He leaned up on his toes for a kiss. "Enjoy finding bouquets and buttonholes."

"Tart. Come on, I'll drop you off."

Kevin and Judith lived in Leeds with their ever-expanding brood of kids. Kevin was a kitchen fitter by public trade and a sadist by private one. He had three regular paying clients who essentially footed the bill for things like family holidays, one other part-time sub like Gabriel that he used for free and a sexual submissive who ruled the roost at home in the form of his wife, Judith.

Gabriel had hooked up with Kevin within weeks of moving up from Sheffield and they had clicked from that very first meeting. They were friends, they were sometimes lovers, they were always family. Kevin was the only man who had rules outside of sex. He was one of only two men who Gabriel trusted completely. And Kevin was, in all ways, Gabriel's safety net. If everything else failed, if absolutely everything else collapsed down around Gabriel's ears, Kevin wouldn't.

Not that Gabriel needed a safety net right now.

He was in a good mood and taunted Aled about flowers all the way into Leeds. It got him kicked out at the end of the street for his crimes, but it was worth it, despite the rain. He jogged up the drive to shelter in the lip of the garage roof that jutted out over the brickwork before rummaging for his key, knowing full well without looking over his shoulder that Aled wouldn't drive off until he'd seen Gabriel go inside. But he wasn't going to knock or dither on the doorstep. No doubt Judith would be busy cooking and Kevin would be busy wrangling the kids—and they were family. What did Gabriel have to knock for?

But he had to find the right bloody key, first.

They'd only just moved to Holbeck—a sorely-needed upgrade after the new baby was born—and Gabriel had had to label the identical keys. He found the silver star sticker for the back door and let himself into the kitchen, walking straight into the warm smell of fresh cream sauce, baking and talcum powder.

"Hello, flower!"

Judith beamed up at him from the table. She was breastfeeding the baby and Gabriel could hear cartoons in the next room. "Kev's just with a client in the workshop. Could you do me a favour and get the pasta on?"

Gabriel smirked, but toed off his shoes and made for the oven. The workshop was a large, soundproofed shed at the bottom of the garden and he and Judith were both here, then any client having any sort of meeting with Kevin in the workshop had to be Sophie. Gabriel had never met her, but she was a high-flying barrister with prison rape fantasies, apparently.

"Is he going to be long?"

"No, it's just a short consultation. Lily! Grace! Come and set your places, please."

The contented feeling of home wrapped around Gabriel's shoulders as the family—his family, even if there was no common blood between them—bustled around him. Pans bubbled. The girls argued about the right way to wash their hands. He tucked his nose against the baby's cheek as he burped her while Judith dished up. Kevin walked someone out to a car, then came in through the front door with his dreadlocks hanging down in thick, wet ropes and donning a huge, white smile when he saw Gabriel holding his youngest.

"Nice to see you, stranger!"

They were just friends in front of the kids. Judith knew exactly what they were and what they did sometimes. No doubt Sophie had heard Gabriel's name as much as he'd heard hers. But in front of the children, who knew nothing about their father's relationships, Gabriel was nothing more than a family friend who worked at fitting bathrooms and kitchens with Dad.

Gabriel didn't mind. In a way, he liked the simplicity. He liked the idea that he *could* just be Dad's friend who helped screw flat-pack kitchens into walls. He was just another man, with no complicated history, nothing that needed explaining.

The baby settled against his shoulder and he went upstairs to put her down for her nap. A couple of turns of the little nursery were all it took, and once she was safely down in her crib and sleeping deeply, he switched on the baby monitor and ducked into Kevin and Judith's room to fetch its counterpart then walked out, and straight into Kevin's hands.

"Hello."

"Up."

Gabriel obediently tipped his head up and closed his eyes at the kiss. Kevin kissed like nobody else. Firm without being sharp. He didn't linger, but it wasn't a chaste peck either. And the hand that was raked through Gabriel's hair made him shiver.

"How you been?"

"Good," Gabriel murmured, then shook himself and gathered his senses again.

"No issues?"

Alcohol, creepy exes, depression, dysphoria...

"Nope. New boyfriend is nice. Another teetotaller."

"Same reason?"

"Nah. Health nut."

Kevin grimaced and Gabriel coughed a quiet laugh.

"He's got a low sex drive, though, so—"

A dark chuckle was his only reply, and Gabriel grinned as it vibrated against his chest. Kevin was nothing like Aled. He was *big.* Over six feet tall, with shoulders as wide as a doorframe and a stern, sharp face that could be terrifyingly sexy under almost any circumstances. And the shadowed confines of an empty landing, with two massive thumbs hooked into Gabriel's waistband and dipping dangerously into his briefs, was definitely the right circumstances.

"You staying tonight?"

"No. Maybe next week," Gabriel said. "Aled's left me sore."

"Good on him."

"Oh, *thanks.*"

"You probably deserved it."

"I fucking w—"

A hand snapped shut around his throat. Gabriel's breath caught. A sudden shock of arousal crashed into his system. Heat flared as lips grazed his ear.

"Mind your fucking language around my fucking kids," Kevin breathed.

Gabriel swallowed thickly. "Yes, sir."

He was slowly released. A deep breath did very little to clear his ragged thoughts. Kevin's hand in his back pocket didn't help matters either. He was sore, but—it hurt so good when Kevin did him. And he didn't have work until two tomorrow. Logic and lust were warring in his head and one was definitely losing.

Then logic lost as Kevin's huge hand slid around the back of his neck and Gabriel was stretched upwards into an immobilising kiss, completely paralysed against the huge frame at his front. Kevin's palm cradled his skull, and he felt fragile and breakable in that hard, heavy grip.

"Stay the night," Kevin whispered against his mouth.

"Okay."

He was dropped. The landing was chilly. Then Kevin's posture shifted almost imperceptibly — the spine bowed a little, the hips relaxed, the cold expression eased — and Gabriel's pounding heart suddenly seemed inappropriate.

"Nice to be home," Kevin said. "I don't think much of Spain."

Gabriel licked his lips. "Ma — Majorca not your thing?"

"Too fucking hot," Kevin muttered. "And Judith's up the duff again, so I had all three of them to myself every morning while she was throwing up. Not much of a holiday."

He laughed shakily. "Put something on the end of it and you wouldn't have this problem."

"She won't let me," Kevin whined. "She wants six. *Six!* Who needs six?"

Gabriel snorted. "Dominant, my arse. She rules you."

"Any more remarks like that, and I *will* dominate your arse."

"Sure," Gabriel said. He winced as a hand the size of a spade slammed into his backside with incredible force, jolting all the aching nerves from Aled's latest game. The spark of pain made him think twice and he fled back to the kitchen for temporary safety.

Lunch had been plated up. He slid into his usual seat and dug in with hopefully more grace than...well, Grace. She and Lily wore more food than they ate, but Gabriel loved the atmosphere. Kevin's family were always happy. Loud and messy and sometimes exasperating and *always* unfathomable, but happy. Gabriel hadn't grown up in one of those families. He only saw his grandfather and uncle nowadays and it was usually awkward and stiff. Lunch at Kevin and Judith's felt more like coming home than lunch at Uncle Chris and Aunt Scott's.

"Next year will be a caravan," Kevin said dramatically, spearing some penne on the end of his fork and waving it at his two daughters. "These two on a plane were a nightmare."

"Come to Cornwall with us," Gabriel said. "Aled's best mate is getting married down there next spring, so we're taking a holiday."

"Oh aye?" Kevin smirked. "That'll be you engaged by the summer, then."

Gabriel gave a dramatic shudder. "I *don't* think so."

"I do. He thinks the world of you. He'll have a ring all ready, you'll see."

"He better not."

"Does Gabriel have a boyfriend?" Grace piped up.

"Yup," Gabriel said.

"Why?"

"Because I love him."

"But why don't you have a girlfriend?"

"Because I love *him,* not a lady," Gabriel said simply.

She eyed him curiously for a moment, then returned to ensuring all the individual pasta pieces in her bowl were quite, quite dead.

"What's wrong with getting married?" Judith asked.

Gabriel shrugged. He wasn't anti-marriage, but…why? What difference did it make? Aled had been married and it had ended in a bitter divorce. Gabriel's mother had never so much as dated any of their fathers, much less married them. Uncle Chris had married Aunt Scott, but nobody had been invited to the wedding and probably for good reason. Marriage just hadn't been a thing for him throughout his life — and given his lifestyle, why add the complication? People made a big deal out of paperwork and wedding rings and Aled probably wasn't going to be his only boyfriend for the rest of his life. What about Kevin? What about Chris? What did marrying Aled say about his relationships with them?

"It's not for me."

That was what it came down to. He didn't want to. It was too many complications, too much money and no decent return. He'd gain nothing and just add a load of headaches to his life. And after the mess that moving in with Aled in the first place had been — coinciding with an abusive ex, a job loss and panicking about being homeless again — Gabriel was done with headaches.

"It makes having kids much easier," Judith said and patted her stomach. "Did Kevin tell you?"

"You're bonkers is what he told me," Gabriel parried. "Anyway, me and Aled aren't having kids. He doesn't want any."

"He might change his mind."

"Doubt it." Not to mention that he couldn't. That was why he'd ended up getting divorced in the first place. His ex-wife had wanted a baby and it had turned out that Aled couldn't produce the goods. On the plus side, it generally made it much easier to persuade Aled to part with the rubbers every now and then once they'd become a regular thing. Her loss, Gabriel's gain. "I don't either."

"And you might change yours!" Judith sang.

Gabriel rolled his eyes but ignored the sting of the remark.

"You can have my share."

"Don't encourage her," Kevin grunted.

"We're thinking of Leah or Leo for this little one."

"You're thinking of Leah or Leo. They're bloody awful. I still think Kevin or Kevinella are perfectly good—"

"No."

Gabriel smirked into his pasta as Judith shot her master down. She was Kevin's submissive and they did more in the way of lifestyle submission than Gabriel was comfortable with—Judith wore a GPS tracker on her chastity belt, and had to ask Kevin for money—but in a way, they were cut from the same cloth as he and Aled. She might be the submissive, but she owned him in reality, just as Gabriel held all the real power in his relationship with Aled.

"What do you think?"

Gabriel swallowed. "Sorry?"

"Leo and Leah."

He glanced between Kevin's exasperated expression and Judith's tight jaw. He liked them. And Kevin wasn't so keen. And after the little display on the landing…

He shifted in his seat, adjusted himself and threw down his cards.

"Leah's cute."

Kevin's expression never faltered, but a foot slid between Gabriel's on the tiles and pushed up. His knees were opened and steadily kicked wider and wider, in a blatant warning, until Kevin's heel rested against his crotch. Hot, hard and dangerous.

Gabriel's jacket was over the back of his chair, and when Judith got up to serve dessert, he fished in the pockets for his phone.

Me: Staying at Kevin's tonight. See you tomorrow x

Chapter Thirteen

Christmas Day was — a *day*.

It arrived out of nowhere, the unyielding winter and competing demands suddenly jarring to a halt on Christmas Eve after a surprise get-out-of-work-free card from the boss and coming home to find that Gabriel had decorated in his absence, up to and including a bauble in a somewhat surprising place as an early present.

So — naturally — Aled punished him the following morning for the inappropriate use of Christmas decorations.

Punishment half-inflicted, Aled found some suitable going-out clothes, shrugged on a jumper and shut the wardrobe door.

"Right, I'm off," he said. "Be good."

Gabriel's only answer was a shaky breath. Aled had been woken up with a hand job, so had taken his revenge by plugging Gabriel with the largest vibrator they owned, trussing him up in ribbons then wrapping the bound body in delicate tissue paper. The duck-egg blue was a sensual counterpoint to the red flush in Gabriel's shivering skin.

He stooped over the bed and kissed the edge of the gag.

"If you're still just like that when I get back, you'll get your Christmas present."

He locked the bedroom door behind him, then headed downstairs whistling jauntily. There was no chance Gabriel would manage it. He could come on that particular dildo when it was switched off, never mind when it delivered a deep, throbbing pulse every two to six seconds. Just predictable enough to keep him on the edge but changing too often to let him zone out and ignore it.

He'd never last. And that meant another punishment. So Aled reversed off the drive in high spirits and sang along to the radio as he headed over to Pontefract.

It wasn't just his turn to visit for Christmas — he took turns with his much-loathed Uncle Paul, so they never had to actually see one another — but he had news to deliver as well. Not only had Aled's parents acted as *de facto* parents for Suze, but Nana had been her nana too. If anything, Suze sometimes saw Nana more often than Aled, especially if work sent him off travelling. They had kept her out of care between them for a good seven or eight years after the dementia had begun, but, in the end, they hadn't been able to provide all the care she needed.

Nana might be in the home now, but she'd still want to know all about Suze's wedding.

Not that Nana was quite gone yet. She had insisted that if she had to go into care, it wasn't going to be too far from her bingo night, hence Pontefract. She'd refused to come to Wakefield to live nearer to them and had rather tartly told Aled that he had a nice car, so needed to shut up moaning about having the opportunity to use it more. He could drive to visit her at the flat and he could drive to visit her at the home.

Bingo was long since gone — or rather, Nana's ability to get there was long gone — but she'd settled in to a new routine in the home and was generally happy enough. She still knitted too much. She constantly whinged about the staff and their inability to make a decent cup of tea. As the dementia had progressed, she *had* developed that uncomfortable habit of making racist remarks now then, but it hadn't got too serious yet. And Aled trusted them to care for her — and that was depressingly hard to come across these days.

So, sure, Pontefract wasn't the most convenient place for her to live anymore. But why change what she loved, or risk her safety for a few miles?

The home itself was a pretty cluster of bungalows around a central building, the bungalows ranging from full nursing care to assisted living like Nana's. It was always busy, and Christmas was definitely not an exception. Aled had to park out on the road, too late to snag a parking space.

"Hello, pet!" the receptionist said cheerily. "Here to see Aggie, are you?"

"Always," Aled said, signing the register. "Merry Christmas."

"And you, pet."

The home looked like a Christmas elf had barfed on it. Nana had a room in an assisted bungalow, only one step down from full nursing care, but even the various machines, trolleys and pulleys had been decorated with bows. Her name plate was framed in tinsel and when Aled knocked and cracked open her door, the assistants had helped her put up all her old ornaments from the house. His earliest memories had featured that very same little tree, and he grinned as he stepped into the room.

"There you are!" she croaked.

Nana was ninety-nine years old. Aled was adopted, so of course she looked nothing like him, but her frail hands on his back were familiar as his own name when he stooped to hug her. He remembered summers playing with Suze on his grandparents' lawn, kicking a ball into Nana's roses and getting the back of his jeans smacked with the carpet brush every time. Now, she couldn't have smacked him with a hanky and she forgot his name more often than not, but enough remained. She remembered enough that her face lit up when he stooped to hug her. She remembered enough that she was pleased to see him. She knew he was family, even if she couldn't always remember if he was Euan or Euan's son.

"No Melissa?"

"No, Nana. We're divorced."

"Oh, yes, that's right. It's a new girl, isn't it? Gabby."

They'd mutually agreed to give up. Nana had taken Gabriel for a girl when they'd first been introduced, then got upset when gently corrected. At first, she'd been upset that the dementia was ruining her ability to recall things properly. Now she'd get upset because she thought they were trying to lie to her. She didn't seem able to realise that it wasn't a question of her memory *or* lies, and Gabriel had grudgingly agreed to just let her think he was a woman.

Which, Aled mused, was probably why he didn't visit much.

"Yep. She's visiting her grandfather today," Aled lied, the false pronouns rolling like heavy marbles on his tongue, unpleasant and awkward.

"Ooh, that's nice of her. Do you like him?"

"Her granddad?" Aled asked. "We've never met. Come on, we got you a present. Open it."

Gabriel had written the card and wrapped it, maybe to make up for skipping out on the visit. The paper was the same duck-egg blue that Aled had used to trap him and he shifted a little uncomfortably as Nana picked at the paper.

"Suze sends her love and says she'll drop by tomorrow," he said as Nana slowly opened her gift. "She's getting married next year. She wants to give you your invitation personally."

"Oh, that would be *lovely*," Nana sighed. "But I don't think I'm up to that sort of thing now, you know."

Aled bit his lip. She was probably right. After her fall last year, she was almost completely bed-bound. He hated to think it, but it was entirely likely that she wasn't going to see her big milestone birthday.

"When are you getting married?" she asked. "Oi! Don't you go interfering! I can open my own present."

He chuckled but sat back again. "I'm divorced now, Nana."

"Not Melissa. Gabby."

He raised his eyebrows. "Gabby? We're not going to get married."

"Why not?" she demanded imperiously.

The end of the soft package finally opened properly, and a silver necklace slithered out into her crooked fingers. She trilled appreciatively and Aled was saved from further questioning for a little while by helping her put it on and fetching the mirror.

"Lovely. Tess, look!" she chirped when the door cracked and the assistant came in with her Christmas dinner on a tray. "Look at my new necklace."

Aled busied himself with rescuing all the splinters of tissue scattered on the bedsheets as Nana and Tess admired the necklace and the tray was set up, then sank back into his seat once the door had closed again — only to discover that Nana had latched on to the idea anyway.

"I can wear it at your wedding," she said brightly. "When's that again?"

"I'm not getting married again, Nana."

"Well, you should," she snapped. "You need a good wife."

Aled smirked. Gabriel would make a bloody awful wife. And in Nana's worldview, Aled had always been more of a wife than even his actual wife. What husband changed the bedsheets, after all?

"I tried that," he said. "I'm not very good at being married."

"You got lazy," she said. "You know better now."

"I still can't have children, Nana."

"Neither could your mum. Plenty of babies out there."

"Mum wanted one, though. Gab — Gabby doesn't. And neither do I."

"Well, then, who's going to look after you when you're my age?" she asked in a triumphant tone, and Aled laughed.

"Nursing home staff?" he suggested. "And Gabby, I expect. H — she's a bit younger than me."

"That much is obvious," Nana said pointedly.

"*Thanks,* Nana."

"Don't you take that tone with me…"

She was finally persuaded off the topic by some Christmas TV and complaints about dry turkey. Aled sat back, toying with the ribbon off her present and looking at the photographs on the windowsill. They helped her with remembering people's names, even though there wasn't anything written on them. His dad and uncle as boys. Nana and Granddad's twentieth wedding anniversary. Mum and Dad's wedding.

Aled pushed himself up from the chair and reached for the wedding photograph.

Suze had once remarked that Gabriel seemed to come out of nowhere. He was so detached from his roots that Aled had no doubt he'd never meet another Lazarri. He'd never met the uncles in Pudsey, or the grandfather who lived with them. Gabriel visited every month, but never for long, and had said it would probably stop once his grandfather passed away. He had siblings, but Aled didn't know their names. He didn't have his mum's phone number, and there'd never been a father in the picture. Gabriel just *was.* His real family were Kevin and Judith, and they were nothing to do with his birth.

In a way, Aled was the same. His father was an ash-blond Welshman built like a rake. His mother was a sharp-nosed Indian woman with a spectacular singing voice. He had always known he was adopted. It had always been so obvious, and yet something that had never really touched him. He had a family. What did he need to know more for?

His birth father was in the wedding photo. Dad's best friend, the best man at his wedding, the partner in crime who'd nudged him when the pretty doctor from cardiology had walked past in the hospital canteen and said, "Time to grow a pair and ask her out, Euan." He had Aled's ginger hair and crooked smile. His name had been David. His girlfriend was Amanda, a primary school teacher from Hebden Bridge. She had worn soft cardigans all the time and made the best sponge cake in all of Yorkshire. He'd owned an old brown Ford car, with a blue flower on the bonnet that she'd painted just to annoy him one summer.

Rainy night, sharp bend and the old Ford had come off the road.

And that was that.

Aled put the photo down and turned to find Nana staring at him through narrowed eyes.

"It doesn't matter, you know," she said.

"What?"

"If you marry Gabby."

"Nana —"

"She's family."

Aled smiled.

Family. Like Kevin and Judith. Like Nana. Like Tom and Suze. Like the people who were nothing to do with how they were made, but everything to do with who they'd become. Like the people who loved them.

* * * *

Aled opened a single eye as the bathroom door opened.

"You still soaking?"

"Yup."

Gabriel shut the door with a snap and slid down to sit on the bathmat, hooking his arms over the edge. He grimaced faintly, and Aled smirked.

"Sore?"

"Bastard."

"You start mouthing off again, I'll do it again."

"That's a definite red," Gabriel muttered. "I feel like my ovaries are going to fall out."

"Oh, please. That's nothing. Wait until you find out what Kevin's got planned for you for New Year."

"Oh, *fuck* – "

"Well, yeah…"

Gabriel laughed, then rocked his head to rest sideways on the edge of the bath. It looked painful as hell, yet he seemed to relax there.

"You all right?" Aled asked.

"Mm. Just got off the phone with my uncle."

"Bad news?"

"I guess," Gabriel said. "My mother is coming up to visit Granddad. Scott was trying to persuade me to see her."

"Fuck that," Aled said. "She's not your family."

Gabriel raised his eyebrows. "Er. She's my – "

"Mother doesn't make her a mum," Aled interrupted. "None of that lot are your family. You don't owe them shit."

"I know," Gabriel said. "I'm not going. Rather let Kevin beat me for real, no safewords. Scott's just – he pulls the guilt trip shit."

"Then to hell with him too. He should know better. You said they drove him out for being gay."

"Guess they've made up."

"Bully for them."

Gabriel stood up and stripped out of his briefs. The savage welts on his arse were a violent red as he dipped a toe into the bath water, then vanished under the bubbles as he sank into the heat with Aled. Aled raised an eyebrow but spread his legs to allow Gabriel to wedge himself between them. The bath wasn't huge, but Gabriel was a skinny wretch, so it was just about manageable. The ring glinted and Aled cupped the guilty breast, gently massaging the weightless curve in the palm of his hand.

"Mm. S'nice…"

Gabriel relaxed against him and Aled brushed his lips along his hairline.

"We got a family right here," he whispered. "Kevin and Judith and Tom and Suze and Nana. You want to go visit someone, go visit them."

Gabriel sighed, and stretched. The water rippled.

"Keep doing what you're doing," he whispered, "and I won't be going nowhere."

Aled chuckled and began to roll the nipple between finger and thumb. He was too tired and full of good food to bother joining in, but he loaned both hands to Gabriel's idle masturbation and watched the reflection of the light off the water dancing on the ceiling. His thoughts drifted along, detached from the softness of the breast in his right or the warmth of the cunt in his left. Nana was right. It didn't matter if they were married. But she was also right in that Gabriel was family. And part of Aled — the part that had got married in the first place, the part that was excited for Suze, the part that believed there was something in marriage — wanted to cement it.

He rocked his hips. He was hard from the lazy playing, and he pushed until Gabriel turned over and sank down onto him. Aled leaned forward to kiss the ring, then sucked it into his mouth and held it between his teeth as Gabriel moved.

There could be another.

Perhaps there should be.

Chapter Fourteen

Aled's birthday was on the fourth of January and Gabriel usually celebrated it on the fifth, with a suitably hungover Aled who probably hadn't got laid the night before. It was a bit of a tradition. Aled's old friends and Gabriel's alcohol problem weren't exactly compatible. It was their workaround. And a very nice one, usually.

So he was more than a little surprised to leave work on the fourth and find Aled waiting in the car.

"No pub crawl with Tom and Suze?" he asked once he'd hooked the bike up to the back and slid into the passenger seat.

"Next weekend," Aled said. "Fancied spending the big day with you instead."

"Yeah?"

"Yep."

"With me, or in me?"

"You say that like they're mutually exclusive," Aled drawled as he peeled out of the carpark and Gabriel grinned.

"So what's the plan?"

"Home and a shower for you first," Aled said pointedly.

"Hey!"

"Then I was thinking dinner somewhere nice and a walk home if it's not too cold?"

Gabriel shivered. He knew what that meant. A nice dinner and a fuck in the dark recesses of some park on the way back. Probably Thornes Park. Under the trees, in the absolute blackness, where it would be cold and dirty and even if they could hear him scream, nobody would come to help him.

"Sounds good."

Aled never bothered to take the day off work for his birthday and badmouthed his boss the whole way home. He followed Gabriel into the bathroom to watch him shower, but Gabriel was just treated to a hug in a bath sheet and a kiss. The nearest thing to an appearance their sex life made was that Aled had laid out clothes for Gabriel to wear, which was usually not part of their lifestyle. Gabriel raised an eyebrow at them. No bra, no binder, no briefs — and a plug sitting proudly atop that godawful chastity belt. Gabriel curled his lip. He *hated* chastity belts. But then he sighed and decided to roll with it just this once. Birthday treats and all that.

"Are we walking to the pub, then?" he asked as he squirmed into the very tight T-shirt.

"We'll get a taxi," Aled said. He looped both arms around Gabriel's hips and slid his hands into his back pockets. Gabriel rose up on his toes for a short kiss that turned out to be somewhat longer. By the time it broke, Gabriel was tempted to hang the whole idea of dinner and skip straight to the dirty fuck.

"Do we *have* to eat?"

Aled chuckled and patted his backside. "Yes. Now come on. Lucy at work was recommending this great new Italian place in town."

"Why the date?" Gabriel asked suspiciously.

"Maybe I wanted to appreciate you for my birthday."

"Maybe you're up to something."

Aled smirked but didn't rise to the bait.

It was freezing out, and Gabriel wasn't allowed anything but his thin leather jacket — and he wasn't allowed to zip it up, either. Walking up into the town centre had never felt so far. Everyone else was smarter than them — the streets were near-deserted, the shops shut and even the busiest bars had their clientele huddled inside rather than smoking in packs on the side of the road like usual. Town was emptier than Christmas morning.

"Where's this Italian place, then?" Gabriel asked as they headed for the cut-through by the cathedral.

"Near the police station."

Gabriel frowned. "Then why did we come this — *hey*!"

The brickwork slammed into his back. Aled's eyes glittered in the dark. The alley was short. Not ten metres away lay the open street. The shadow of the cathedral plunged them into darkness from the other side of the brick arch.

Gabriel's heart raced.

It was like how they'd first met. Messages on Grindr and a brutal shag between a couple of dumpsters on the way back to Gabriel's place. He'd been wet within seconds then, too. And the hard, predatory look on Aled's face in the gloom wasn't helping matters.

Aled leaned in and whispered a single word.

"Quiet."

The button and zip on Gabriel's jeans parted like butter under a knife. His knees did too. The scrape of denim on his legs sent prickles of lust back up them. The rough edge of brick on his bare arse was even better. The slide of the key into the belt made Gabriel bite his lip, imagining it as a hollow echo of the slide of Aled's dick into him in just a few short moments.

But it didn't work out like that.

Instead, Aled followed the jeans down. In the cold damp of a Yorkshire alleyway, his mouth was the searing heat of paradise. He blew first — quite literally. Just blew a gentle, warm breeze down the length of Gabriel's swollen cock, against the closed lips, into the creases of thighs and the crooked twists of hair. Two kisses were offered to Gabriel's hip bones, then lips touched his own and gently but persistently parted them. A burning tongue caressed the underside of his cock, almost like it could be pulled free of its surroundings and exposed. Gabriel tilted his hips to help, only for hands to grip him tight and hold him still.

"Please — "

"*Quiet.*"

He held his tongue as Aled let his own loose. Stroking. Smoothing. Almost soothing but for the intense heat. One moment a tiny point touching the very tip of him, and the next surrounding him entirely. He tightened his grip on the plug as Aled's work — and Gabriel's want — made it harder and harder to hold on to. It failed when Aled sealed his lips around Gabriel's cock and sucked so hard that the world wobbled out of view.

The chuckle nearly shattered him, then wet silicone was pressed into the palm of his hand.

"Hold on to that."

"O-okay —*fuuu*—"

Hands grabbed his knees when they buckled. Blindly chasing the high, Gabriel shoved a hand up his shirt and began to play with his nipple ring. He felt hollow. Everything was speeding up. Aled's sucking. His hand on Gabriel's knee. The other — the other —

Gabriel came with a ragged gasp as two wide fingers were shoved into him, plunging until a palm grazed the root of his cock. He slid down into it as the climax smashed through him and came back to himself with most of a hand inside him, his jeans tangled around his shins, and a chuckling mouth sucking kisses into one exposed boob.

"Stayed quiet," he whispered hoarsely.

"You did. Well done."

The hand withdrew. Cool silicone replaced it, then the belt was locked back into place. Gabriel tasted his own sweetness on Aled's fingers when he was made to suck them clean.

"That's why we came the long way around," Aled murmured, and dragged Gabriel to his feet. His jeans were ripped up and buttoned. His T-shirt was pulled back into place. "Now we're going to dinner, and you can return the favour."

"W-what?"

"At dinner," Aled said. "They've got long tablecloths."

Gabriel's jaw sagged. Aled wanted a birthday blow job in the middle of a busy restaurant?

"You're kidding."

"No. But if you'd rather not—" Aled's hand trailed to Gabriel's arse and tugged it, and him, away from the brick. "Then there's always the men's toilets."

He squeezed one cheek. Pleasure crackled outwards like fire. Gabriel thought furiously as he was kissed. Suck Aled off under a table in a busy restaurant, or get bent over a sink — likely in the same restaurant — and dry-fucked without making a sound. One was tricky. The other was downright impossible.

And neither were what Aled was really up to.

Gabriel knew a distraction when he saw it — and he wanted to see it to the end.

"Fair's fair," he said, and crossed his fingers for luck.

* * * *

Gabriel had a mouth full of hard, leaking cock when the shoes approached the table.

"Would you like to see the dessert menu, sir?"

The restaurant had been busy all evening, but Aled had booked a secluded booth at the back. The booth was high and only the waiters bothered about looking at anybody else. It had been easy to pick a moment just after the main course was finished to slide beneath the table unseen — but delivering a blow job in total silence was proving more challenging than Gabriel had expected.

And sucking Aled off mere feet from other oblivious diners much *hotter* than Gabriel had expected.

"My partner's just nipped to the toilets," Aled said smoothly above him. "I'm sure he won't be long."

"Of course, sir. I'll come back."

"Thank you."

The hint spurred Gabriel to action. He'd tried to return the favour properly and take his time, but Aled was already hard as iron in his mouth. Breathing in deeply through his nose, Gabriel opted for the brutal but always effective approach, and readied himself to choke on cock for most certainly not the first time in his life.

At least this time, Aled wasn't going to thrust into it.

But being forced down onto dick, and forcing himself down onto dick, were markedly different things. It was a stop-start of relaxing his throat, moving half an inch and gagging. Then starting all over again. By the time the head was driven down past his throat and finally choked him, Gabriel could feel the sweat on the back of his neck. He wanted Aled to push him the rest of the way. He wanted someone to make him do it and make it all easier. He wanted to be *forced*.

Said a lot, really.

He didn't have the luxury of time now. He'd reel when he pulled off. Loudly. He had to finish things, or they'd both get caught—and Gabriel didn't fancy getting arrested for gross indecency. Blinking back panic and forcing away the dark spots in the corners of his vision, he slowly tensed his throat once more and hummed.

And the trick worked.

Of course it worked. And it worked too well. Without a single sound or movement above him, Aled reached his limit. His cock jumped like a live wire and Gabriel silently retched as the tiny sliver of air he had was drowned in cum. His eyes watered. He pulled back and grimaced as he was struck full in face with his own work.

But silently.

Quiet.

Slowly, he tucked the spent cock away and cleaned his face with a corner of tablecloth. With Aled giving no signal, he had to trust to luck to slide back up into his seat — and he was lucky.

Ish.

Aled tapped the corner of his mouth and Gabriel wiped away the last traces of cum just in time before the waiter bustled back out of the kitchen, saw him and flapped a menu in their direction.

"Dessert, sirs?"

"I'm full, I think," Gabriel said.

"Well, I've got a little bit more room," Aled said with a smirk. "It'll have to be the fudge cake for me. With extra whipped cream."

Gabriel flushed hotly, but waited until the waiter had vanished again before leaning across the table.

"So are you going to tell me what that was about?"

Aled raised his eyebrows.

"You skipped your birthday binge-drinking for a blow job?"

"I skipped it for you," Aled said simply.

"Yeah. Why."

Aled laughed. "Maybe I wanted to spend time with the most important person in my life."

Gabriel squinted suspiciously. "Are you trying to talk me into knives again?"

The laugh softened. Aled slid sideways around the booth to kiss his cheek then slid back.

"I wanted to spend my evening with you," he said again. "The sex is just a nice side effect."

Gabriel narrowed his eyes one last time. That wasn't what was going on. Or if it was, it wasn't the whole story.

"Fine," he said. "Don't tell me."

"Fine by me."

"Happy birthday," he groused, "and I'm never doing that again."

Aled simply held up the key to the belt and admired it in the light.

"Bastard," Gabriel hissed.

"Yes," Aled said, "but I'm the bastard who owns you."

Gabriel instantly felt unpleasantly warm, and distinctly wet. He swallowed back the insult he wanted to throw Aled's way. He was wet and hollow and seriously turned on — but he wanted another side street, not another sadism session.

"Yes, sir."

Aled's smirk widened into a full beam of obnoxious arrogance.

"So mind your manners."

Gabriel swallowed. The bitter aftertaste on his tongue slid away down his throat to join the rest of it. The belt pinched and Gabriel wanted out of it. Preferably in the men's toilets, bent over a sink, staring himself in the flushed face as Aled fucked him raw from behind.

"Yes, sir."

Chapter Fifteen

Life—slightly older life, but much the same life—rolled on.

Grimly.

His birthday was followed by a deluge that made the Book of Noah look significantly more realistic, in Aled's view. Suze's wedding plans took her off down to Cornwall almost every weekend, but the constant rain and occasional apocalyptic hailstorm left him without much to do in her absence except work, fuck, sleep, repeat. To top it off, the weather had Gabriel moody. If work didn't knacker Aled completely for the weekends, then Gabriel's antsy mood certainly had him fucked out by Friday nights.

But he couldn't help but feel like things were changing anyway.

Like the day he got formally invited to his best friend's wedding, put his house up for sale and was confronted by the evidence—yet again—that Gabriel was always changing while Aled never quite managed to stay the same.

It was on a Thursday. Like all the days since his birthday, it was *pissing* it down, and the lock wasn't working properly. The front door finally gave after ten minutes of swearing and fighting with it, and Aled stumbled into the hall and out of the pouring rain for the last time. He didn't care if Gabriel suddenly professed an urge to indulge in knifeplay in the middle of the main road — Aled was *not* going back out in that mess.

"I'm home!" he shouted, tossing his keys into the bowl and stooping to pick up the post. A thick cream-coloured envelope with a red ribbon was in the mix, and he sifted it out with a grin. Wedding invitation. "Gabriel? Did the valuers come?"

"Bedroom!"

Aled headed upstairs with the envelope to find Gabriel changing the sheets. He raised an eyebrow.

"Visitor?"

Originally, Aled had been uncomfortable with the idea of Gabriel bringing his conquests home, but he was trying to shake the habit. Wasn't like he didn't know what Gabriel got up to with the likes of Kevin and Greg anyway. But Gabriel usually texted him to let him know what he'd come home to find, so the sight of him fluffing pillows without a customary message threw him for a moment.

"Nah. Just had a laundry day after I got back from visiting Granddad," Gabriel said. He tossed the last pillow into place and bounced down onto the duvet. "What's that?"

"Wedding invitation. Did the valuers come round?" Aled asked as he ripped open the envelope.

"Yep. I left the quotes on the kitchen counter. They didn't mean much to me."

"Ballpark figures?"

"Between a hundred and ten and a hundred and thirty."

"Like hell it'd get a hundred and thirty," Aled muttered, but nodded. "That'll do. Cover a good high-end flat, that will."

"You want a flat?"

"Yeah. Unless you —"

"No, just surprised," Gabriel said. "You know I don't mind as long as I've got somewhere for the bike, and a nice big bed. You'll just have to gag me more often."

"How terrible," Aled drawled. "Hey, check this out. Suze has addressed this to both of us."

"So?"

"Mr A and Mr G Evans?"

Gabriel snorted. "Like hell. If we ever got hitched, you'd be a Lazarri. My last name is far better. Only decent thing my mum ever gave me."

Aled snorted with laughter and flipped open the invitation.

Dear Aled and Gabriel,

We would be honoured if you would attend the ceremony and celebration of our marriage, to be held at 13:00 on the 2nd of May at The Grand Sea View, St Ives, Cornwall. Please RSVP confirming your attendance as soon as possible.

Much love,

Tom and Suze

"I'm guessing she wants to collect the replies," Aled said. "Should I write something nice or abusive?"

"Abusive," Gabriel said.

"I'll blame you."

"That's fine. She won't believe you."

Aled wrinkled his nose.

"Can we have wedding sex?" Gabriel asked, flopping back to sprawl out on the bed.

"I was assuming that was a given."

"I've always wanted to fuck a best man," Gabriel said dreamily.

"Yeah? Why haven't you?"

"Never get invited to weddings," Gabriel replied. "Do you?"

"Occasionally. Work colleagues and their evening dos to prop up numbers, usually. Never been a best man."

"Have fun."

"If you don't mind out, we'll stuff you in a dress and call you a bridesmaid."

"Too far," Gabriel snapped.

Aled winced at the vehement tone. "Sorry." He dropped the invite onto the bedstand and stooped to kiss Gabriel's cheek. He was thrown another foul look but mollified it with a proper kiss on the mouth. "Hey. It's pissing it down outside. Want to cosy up in the conservatory chair with a blanket and read?"

"Rather cosy up in the conservatory chair with a blanket and have sex."

Aled snorted with laughter. "Well, you might have to persuade me into it. Knackered after too many meetings today."

"Corporate life getting to you?"

"Corporate life has *always* gotten to me," Aled said. He started to work at his tie, eyeing his reflection in the mirror. Even he had to admit that he looked tired. "I didn't go into marketing because I like selling things to people."

"I don't even know what you sell," Gabriel said.

"Whatever the customer wants us to sell. Usually legal and accountancy services."

"Sounds *thrilling*," Gabriel drawled. "At least selling gym memberships I get to slag off people's husbands with them."

"And ogle naked men."

"Can do that whenever I want," Gabriel said, pointedly rolling over and propping his chin on his hand to watch Aled take off his shirt. Aled smirked and did a little hip shimmy before unbuckling his belt. So what if it was more of a belly dance than a sexy slide? It was nice to be appreciated sometimes. Aled wasn't an idiot—he knew full well that he'd caught Gabriel's attention by being an exciting fuck and held it by being good company otherwise. He'd been the same with his ex-wife, and indeed anybody else who'd ever looked his way. Nobody had ever hit on him for being handsome. He wasn't physically anything to write home about. But he didn't have to be, and he proved it by rolling Gabriel over by the shoulders, running both palms flat down that long, sleek belly, and straight into his underwear.

"Make yourself useful, then," he said.

Aled preferred to get a blow job in a power grab, and to give one with Gabriel chained to the headboard and his legs held painfully wide. But sixty-nining was good too, and he didn't feel the need to play. His own climax was mild and relatively unimportant. Gabriel's was a shudder and a sigh and Aled cleaned his tongue off by leaving wet kisses from hip to hairline before stepping away from the bed again and flicking Gabriel's shirt back down with a lazy movement of the wrist.

"How about that cuddle in the conservatory, then?"

"Mm, okay."

He took his tablet and sent instructions to commence a house sale to his chosen solicitor while Gabriel made a couple of brews. The rain was drumming on the roof in a hypnotic fashion, and Aled wasn't too surprised when Gabriel climbed into the chair next to him, draped himself over Aled's lap in an artful manner and promptly fell asleep. Aled just sat and stroked a bare foot and went flat-shopping online.

The truth was, he didn't want a flat. Not long term. But the house was increasingly feeling like a relic from a life he didn't recognise anymore. A time when he'd been someone's husband, and all their quirks and kinks had been invisible and under the surface. There had never been anything on display, like the locks on the outside of the spare room door or the alarm cord in the bathroom that served as a safeword. Gabriel had been the first to raise the idea of getting their own place, but it had grown on Aled.

But he wanted another flat.

Because the fact was that his best friend was moving away. Suze had been a cornerstone of Aled's life for as long as he could remember. His home had always been where Suze was. He had keys to her house, and she to his. They'd lived together in university. They'd been on holidays together before he got married. Even when Melissa had been uncomfortable with how close he was to Suze, he'd never listened.

He wasn't sure that—with Suze going away—he would retain an attachment to Wakefield without her. The only other thing that he breathed for here was Gabriel. And Gabriel—

Even six months ago, Aled would have laughed at the idea of Gabriel moving half the country to stay with him, but it felt less ridiculous now. Maybe he would.

Maybe he wouldn't. Maybe they could work something out, some kind of halfway compromise like Birmingham or Bristol.

But if they had a flat, then they could transfer it into a buy-to-let mortgage and rent it out rather than go through the whole rigmarole of selling up and buying again. Get on the rental property ladder and start building up his investments. After all, Aled didn't want to have to work forever, and Gabriel—much as he was the best thing to walk into Aled's life since his wife had walked out of it—was not exactly a financially wise option. Mopping floors and scanning key fobs at the gym didn't pay many bills.

Aled squeezed the foot captured in his hand and smiled at the floorplan of a nice new-build out by the hospital.

A spacious flat for the time being.

They could work on another house some other time.

* * * *

Gabriel materialised in the kitchen halfway through Aled's prep and took over chopping the tomatoes without a word.

"Hello to you too," Aled said, and kissed the side of his head as he shifted around to get to the pans. The kitchen really was too small for both of them to work in it, but he liked the closeness when the weather was so dark and foul outside. "Kevin rang while you were napping."

Gabriel had woken up when Aled had escaped but had simply migrated to the sofa and gone back to sleep. Aled had left him to it and stolen the phone when it started ringing.

"Am I in trouble?"

"Nah. He was going to invite you round for dinner. Judith was making carbonara."

"Aw, I missed her special carbonara?" Gabriel whined.

"She'll box some up for you."

"I'm working tomorrow."

"I can pick it up on my way home."

That earned him a fly-by kiss on Gabriel's way to the fridge for a couple of peppers. Aled leaned up against the oven, stirring the pot occasionally, and caught him on the way back for a proper one.

"I wanted to ask you about Kevin, actually," Gabriel said, putting the peppers aside but then returning to Aled's grip.

"Oh?"

"I've been wanting to try something for a while now and I wanted to know how you'd feel about doing it with me and Kevin."

"Definite 'it.'"

"Double penetration."

Aled raised his eyebrows. "Of you, I hope."

Aled wasn't into taking it. He'd tried a few times with Melissa using toys, and maybe twice with other men, but it just didn't do anything for him.

"Yeah."

Aled blew out his cheeks and smoothed his hands down Gabriel's arms. "Sorry," he said. "But while I'm totally up for handing you over between us, actually getting involved with your sex with Kevin isn't something I'm really up for."

Gabriel sighed, but looped his arms around Aled's neck and kissed his cheek. "Okay."

"It's just a bit too close quarters," Aled said. "I like him as a person, I trust him with you in that sort of situation, but—the kind of things you like to do together, I wouldn't feel comfortable."

Gabriel nodded. "I get it."

"Maybe if you roped in one of your more vanilla conquests," Aled offered. "If I'm a little bit more in control of the situation with you and someone more straightforward than Kevin, then maybe we can work something out."

"Okay," Gabriel said and sidestepped to get back to the peppers. "I've just wanted to try it for a while. It's just that Kevin does DP sometimes with his other subs, but the guy he partners with for it gives me the creeps. I tapped out of the one scene he was invited to."

"What was wrong with him?"

"No idea. I just didn't like him. Judith thinks he's wonderful but he was a bit...I don't know. It felt *too* real with him. Like even when you or Kevin are at your scariest, I know it's not *really* real. I'm not *really* scared. But with him...yeah, it was real fear. So I tapped out. And I mean, he stopped, he stopped the minute I told him to, Kevin didn't have to step in or anything but yeah, we don't play. So I talked to Kevin about it but Dave's the only guy he does that with, so it was a dead end."

"Fair enough," Aled said. "I mean, I think Greg's an idiot but for one night I'd be willing to do it with him."

"Greg wouldn't. He's scared of you."

Aled blinked. "He's never seen me."

"He has. I showed him a picture. He used to work at the security desk in your building. Last year, maybe the year before? He said he saw you once in a slanging match with some other suit and it made his balls crawl up into his body and die."

Aled burst out laughing. "Fucking hell. That would have been Callahan."

"Who?"

"Absolute fuckwit who used to run Sales until he got caught stealing office supplies and sacked. I wasn't the only one who bawled him out in public." Aled relished the memory. It had been one of the few very pleasant parts of working there—*everyone* had hated Callahan, so there was no other friction when he was about. He remembered the row, too. He'd only gone toe-to-toe with him once, and his boss's response had simply been to please refrain from swearing so much on the office floor, now where were they on the new digital campaign strategy.

"Well apparently you were terrifying and Greg refused to get involved to split it up so he got sacked too."

"I did wonder why nobody stepped in," Aled said, smirking. "Small world. If I'm so scary, why's he stayed with you?"

"I showed him some text messages where I outright told you I was shagging him."

"Fair enough," Aled said, moving aside as Gabriel added the tomato and peppers to the pan. "Get some salad out to go with this, would you?"

"Sure."

"So Greg is too scared to get his dick out near me, I'm guessing Chris isn't going to be up for it and Kevin's mate is too scary for you."

"And I'm not doing it with a stranger," Gabriel finished. "Do you know anyone at your club who would do it?"

"Not anymore," Aled said. "We'd quickly find someone if we went more regularly, though."

Gabriel hummed, but didn't sound too enthusiastic.

"Unless you don't want to go to the club again?" Aled asked.

"Jury's still out. It was great, but...I don't know. I think it's more I expect there to be problems. You know. Different plumbing and all that."

"Ah."

"Guess I need to go hunt around some fetish forums and make a few friends."

"Not Grindr?"

"Gone off it a bit, to be honest," Gabriel said. "I'm sick of explaining how I'm a man with tits and a box. I don't have to bother with you and Greg and Kevin and Chris. And it's been a long time since I was on the fetish forums, but they were always less bothered."

"Well, think on it," Aled said and caught a hip to drag him in and kiss a shoulder. "I will ask that you let me know if you're going to do it with two other people. You and one newcomer is fine, but you and two on your own is a bit much."

"It won't be that way around," Gabriel said flatly. "I want *someone* who knows what he's doing with me."

Aled laughed and kissed the other shoulder.

"Plenty of them about," he said. "Think on it. And I'll do the same. And we'll see what we can do."

Chapter Sixteen

Gabriel had spent a sunny weekend cycling in the Cotswolds with Chris, so wasn't too surprised to get back on Sunday evening to a deluge and road closure that took him the long way home. He was already exhausted from trying to keep up with Chris, and by the time he let himself in, he felt not just like a drowned rat, but one that had been clubbed half to death first.

"Aled!" he shouted. "Can we play?"

Silence. He huffed, checked the key bowl and figured that, despite the car on the drive, Aled had gone out. Probably drinking with Tom and Suze if he'd left the car behind. Great. And Kevin was never available on Sunday evenings *and* Greg wasn't the kinky type anyway. Gabriel didn't want sucking off. He wanted to be compressed, trapped, *squeezed*. Getting off would be nice, but it wasn't mandatory.

And there was nobody around to do it.

He went foraging instead. The takeaway menus were uninspiring. The freezer was empty. But the fridge held baked gold in the form of cake. Boxes upon boxes, all with only one or two slices each. Seven different bakeries were represented there, and Gabriel puzzled over them until he found a fruit slice with white icing like a Christmas cake and figured it out. Wedding cake samples. Obviously Aled had lost the argument about the weekend plans.

He took a slice into the living room and kicked up his feet on the sofa. He wanted a wank but felt too tired to do anything about it. He shrugged out of his clothes but didn't get any further and moodily munched on the cake as he stared blindly at some random TV show. He couldn't have named it if he'd been paid.

And the next thing he knew, there was a hand tipping his head back by the chin and a familiar mouth on his own.

"'Lo."

"Hello," Aled said with a chuckle. "Good time in the Cotswolds?"

"Mm."

"Want anything to eat?"

"Got cake."

"Anything that counts as real food."

"Cake is real food," Gabriel said muzzily, then blinked himself properly awake. He still had half a slice, but it had gone dry and disgusting so he abandoned it on the coffee table. "Where've you been?"

"Just walked down to Asda."

"In the rain?"

"Wasn't raining when I left," Aled said.

Gabriel twisted over on the sofa and knelt up on the cushions. Aled was still stooping against the back, leaning on his elbows, and Gabriel nudged his way between them for a close, intimate kiss.

"I want to play," he whispered.

156

Aled chuckled. "You always want to play after you've seen Chris."

"I'm exhausted. I wanted to be squeezed up tight until I can hardly breathe, then fucked into a coma."

"Very romantic," Aled drawled. "And why should I bother?"

"You can fuck me."

"I can fuck you whenever I want."

The arrogance brought his dick to life just like that. Gabriel licked his lips enticingly, but Aled's gaze never wavered.

"You can do me with a condom."

"I can do that whenever I want too."

Gabriel kissed him. He coaxed Aled open, trying to tempt him. But Aled was a frustratingly well-controlled dominant sometimes, and he gave nothing away.

But Gabriel had an ace up his sleeve.

"I'll let you rent me out to someone at your club."

Aled pulled back a little. His eyes narrowed. Gabriel waited hopefully. The idea was still scary as hell, but he would be safe in Aled's hands.

"I'll let you hold me down while someone else fucks me," he whispered. "And it'll be so scary and so hot and you can pick whoever and whenever you want."

"You get one chance to back out of that deal," Aled said. "Because I'll hold you to it."

Gabriel jutted out his chin and said nothing.

"Deal," Aled said. "Now go upstairs and get dressed. Pyjama bottoms, briefs, socks, bra, T-shirt, hoodie. And get my dressing gown. Then come back down."

"Hoodie?"

"Do it."

"Yes, sir."

He vanished upstairs but had to rummage for everything he needed. He didn't own any hoodies of his own anymore and Aled's old university one could be worn as a short dress. It smelled like him even though Gabriel had never seen him wear it, and he tucked his nose into the sleeve for a second before heading back downstairs.

Aled hadn't really done much in his absence. He'd kicked off his shoes and was channel-surfing. Gabriel tucked himself up onto the cushions beside him and settled in for a cuddle until Aled found something he wanted to watch.

"Right. Get up."

Gabriel rose, and stood mute as Aled bound his wrists with one end of the dressing gown cord and tied the other around his neck. The hood was flipped up then Aled's dressing gown draped around his shoulders and the empty sleeves tied across his front. He was trapped before he was ever tipped down to lie on his front on the sofa. The dressing gown was bunched up around his waist, and his pyjamas and briefs pulled to his knees.

Then the weight came down.

Gabriel breathed out in a long, luxurious sigh as Aled settled along his back. He was forced down into the cushions. Imprisoned. Crushed. Suffocated. *Surrounded.* He couldn't have fought his way out if he'd tried. He was completely helpless.

It was compounded by the hand that came down on the side of his head. He gasped, and fingers invaded his mouth. They dragged on his tongue and pushed in until he gagged before withdrawing a fraction.

"Suck them."

He sealed his lips and sucked, toying with the short nails and smooth whorls. The hand on his head eased. Hot breath touched his cheek, and Gabriel shivered as his ear was enveloped in wet heat and the shell dragged between sharp teeth.

For a while, that was all there was. Heat. Wetness. The shivering arousal of a mouth playing with his ear. The fingers slowly withdrew and toyed with his lips like they were labia — teasing them out, rubbing them, dragging nails dangerously around the seams, dipping in and out in idle prods and probes. Somehow, Gabriel knew the hand wasn't going to be used to make it easier on him, and the knowledge only made him wetter. He'd not need help.

But the cold air when Aled finally sat back and parted him with both hands was still a shock and Gabriel flinched.

"Make a sound and I'll gag you."

He clenched his jaw — and his cunt — as Aled pushed in. The sparks of pain filled his cock and he ground down into the cushions as he was slowly, inexorably, *painfully* parted around that hot dick. It drove into him in a slow and deliberate push, until he was breathless long before Aled sagged back over him and settled again.

"Looks like sluts can learn to shut up after all."

Gabriel gasped wordlessly at the sudden flood of arousal and Aled's hand sliding between him and the cushions didn't help. A wet thumb rubbed over Gabriel's aching cock, and he almost came from that single stroke. then it happened again, and again, and *again* —

Then he *did* come. Hard. So hard that his spine snapped straight in the intense heat that he'd been drifting in. The rocking of the fuck vanished. *Everything* vanished. There was no rhythm. No pattern. Just him, coming apart in the centre of the world.

And — slowly — coming back together.

His cunt was soaking wet and hollow, like it had dissolved and was ready to pour out of him the moment he stood up. He groaned as the cock in his arse withdrew a fraction, only to push farther in. The pain grounded him. Gathered him back together. Between the wet hand toying with his nipple, hot and invading between his bra and his breast, and the agonisingly dry cock forcing his arse apart, the shattered seams were sewn back together until he was right back where he'd started.

Trapped in a prison of cloth and cushions, pinned between the immoveable object and the unstoppable force, only able to lie there and take the cock driving into him over and over.

"You're dripping wet," a dark voice purred in his ear. "You came so hard that it was like fucking a bowl of soup."

Finger and thumb tightened around his nipple. The cushions were rubbing against his cock. Too rough, too dangerous, too —

"Now."

It tripped another. A ripple of electricity through his dick and hips and spine. From far away, he heard the humiliating sound. His face burned as he was fucked through it in slow, dry movements that prevented him lying to himself. He'd got off like a burst water main. Twice — and once on command.

"*Very* good," the voice whispered, and his tit was squeezed until it ached. "But that's two for you, and none for me. You *owe* me."

The cock inside his arse pressed impossibly deeper — then was pulled out. For a dizzying moment, he was completely hollow. Dragged back onto his knees by the clawed hand squeezing his tit. A finger was shoved into his soaked cunt, and a dismissive tut made his face burn all over again.

"That'll not be fun for me. Better relax."

Pressure against his arse. A hand in the centre of his back. Pressing him down. *Down,* until his face was rammed into the cushions and his arse was totally exposed. The pressure got worse. Gabriel gulped a hungry breath, and relaxed.

Then —

Pain exploded up his leg. Unexpected pain. *Bad* pain. The world blinked out under a wave of bright white agony. His back bowed as though it didn't belong to him. His foot wrenched sideways. Bones ground together with a sickening crunch. Something was wrong. Something was *bad.* Gabriel clawed for breath, tore his consciousness against the pain and reached for the only anchor that he had.

"Red."

Chapter Seventeen

"Red."

The lust burning in Aled's veins turned to ice. He pulled out, instinct lifting his hands away from Gabriel's body. *Let go. Let go. Game over, game over, game over.*

Then he saw the problem.

Not a boundary. Not a word said wrong. Not a hand too heavy, or a phrase too dangerous. No triggers. No dysphoria. Nothing that he had done.

No, the problem was the twisting ripple of contorted muscle running up the back of Gabriel's leg.

"Oh fuck, oh my God, Aled, *please* —"

"Hey, hey, hey," Aled said, dragging the pyjama bottoms and briefs up. "It's okay. Game over. Let me just —"

Gabriel howled as he laid hands on the afflicted leg, then gasped and sagged as Aled twisted. The muscle rebelled, then relaxed just as suddenly as it had cramped.

"Fuck!"

"It's all right," Aled murmured, squeezing hard when the muscle tried to repeat its trick. "Just breathe for me. Just relax. Let's get this under control, then I'll let you out, all right?"

"Mm."

Gabriel's voice was very thin and close to tears. Anxiety tightened in Aled's gut out of sheer instinct — *he'd done that, he'd done that* — but he forced it down. It wasn't his first safeword. It wouldn't be the last. And as safewords went, it wasn't even a dangerous one to deal with.

It was just a bloody cramp.

Aled fought the seizing muscle for some ten minutes before it finally eased, and a pattern of bruises was bound to emerge. But Gabriel finally stopped sobbing into the pillows, and he sagged bonelessly out of the cords and clothes when Aled unwrapped him. The dressing gown was soaked in cold sweat, but he rocked into Aled's hold anyway and Aled squeezed tight, still massaging the leg draped awkwardly across his thigh. The game was long gone. And despite Gabriel's ragged breathing and the ruins of their plans, so was the anxiety.

Oddly, Aled wanted to laugh.

Force him down, wrap him up, almost choke him, fuck him so it hurt, tell him he had no choice — and what got Gabriel to say no?

Cramp.

"I think you need a hot shower," he said. "How many miles did you *go* with Chris?"

"I lost track," Gabriel said hoarsely. "Fuck. Oh my fucking God. That was the worst — *Jesus.* It hurt less the first time I got fisted."

"Kevin?" Aled guessed as he eased the leg off his knees. "Come on. Shower. It'll help."

"Jim, actually."

"Who?"

"First boyfriend."

"Oh, the Sheffield lad," Aled said. Gabriel staggered as he tried to stand and Aled rolled his eyes, catching him under the arms. "All right, come on."

"I was *enjoying* that," Gabriel complained petulantly as Aled helped him up the stairs.

"So was I," Aled said. "You coming all over me like that was hot as hell. Definitely going to try that trick again sometime."

"Arse," Gabriel muttered, blushing hotly.

Aled just chuckled as he sat Gabriel down on the closed toilet and turned on the shower. The muscle was tightening again, and Aled knelt to work at the knots before they could make another go of it. There was a savage bulge in the calf that probably wasn't helping matters, and he worked steadily at it while Gabriel audibly ground his teeth.

"I told you cycling is daft."

"Oh, no, I should swim instead. Then I'll drown if I get a cramp, not just fall off a bike."

"I never get cramp," Aled said loftily.

"Your idea of a workout is four laps of breaststroke then an hour in the hydrotherapy pool."

"I'm noting everything you say," Aled said coolly, "and you will be punished for every last remark once this is sorted out."

"Shove it."

"And that one."

Gabriel's sour mood was helped by a hot shower and a hot water bottle and, within the hour, Aled had

Gabriel established in their bed with the complaining leg stretched out on a pillow, the electric blanket spread out under him like a picnic blanket and the hot water bottle warding off any further surprises. A cup of sweet tea, because sweet tea cured everything, vanished within a few seconds of its delivery, and the empty cup returned with an imperious wave of the hand.

"Another."

"Yes, sir," Aled said mockingly and was flipped off.

He didn't bother with a second. He rinsed the cup out, then puttered around downstairs, throwing their ruined clothes in the wash and locking up for the night. By the time he came back up, Gabriel was half-asleep and drowsy, flicking through TV channels and staring blindly at the offerings through half-lidded eyes.

He looked alluring as hell.

"You didn't get to finish," he murmured.

"Not the first time," Aled said, climbing out of his clothes. He opted just for his briefs, figuring the bed was going to get obscenely hot.

"So?" Gabriel asked, patting Aled's crotch as Aled took off his glasses. "I c'd suck you off from here."

"Maybe in the morning," Aled said. "The mood gets kind of ruined when you say that particular colour."

Gabriel accused him of exaggerating. Aled ignored it. The colours were so ingrained that it really was a mood killer. Gabriel had nearly laughed himself sick last summer when they'd been having perfectly vanilla sex with the TV on, and an advert for Red Bull had stopped Aled dead in his tracks. Pavlov would be proud.

"I take it from the cake in the fridge that the wedding planning isn't finished?"

"What?" Aled asked, surprised by the change of subject.

Gabriel rolled into him and wriggled under his arm, repeating the question. Aled squeezed, kissing the top of his head before settling again.

"Wedding planning isn't finished until you're married," Aled said drowsily.

"What's she got to drag you to next?"

"Oh, God knows. I think the dragging to stuff is done, but the bitching and moaning won't be. Her future mother-in-law is a nightmare."

"So you're going to be on best friend duties until the big day?"

"Pretty much." Aled yawned. "They're in the middle of selling up the house, too. And she handed her notice in last week. So they'll probably move down to Cornwall before the big day, and that'll be dramatic as well."

"She knows phones exist, right? And that Cornwall isn't…I don't know, New Zealand?"

Aled shrugged. "You wouldn't understand. You weren't close to your family."

"I guess so," Gabriel murmured. His voice was a little wistful and Aled squeezed.

"She feels a bit like I would if you moved to the other end of the country," he clarified. "I could still see you. But I'd miss you anyway."

Gabriel stretched. The kiss that landed on Aled's chin was soft and sweet.

"Me too," he whispered.

"Yeah?"

"Yeah. I'm sorry about all the drama of me moving in."

"S'fine."

"If I *was* monogamous, it'd be you," Gabriel said, burrowing his head against Aled's shoulder a little. "I think I'm falling in love with Chris, and Kevin will always be a big part of my life, but — they aren't you. I want you too, no matter who else comes around."

That more than anything made Aled's heart melt a little around the edges. He rubbed his thumb over the space on his ring finger, no longer pale like it had been when he'd finally taken the ring off. In Gabriel's flat of all places. The man who'd helped him let go, and the man he'd had to persuade to hang on.

But Aled didn't see the romance or the love in *needing* someone. It meant far more that Gabriel *wanted* him. Need was as though there were other reasons than love to stay there. Money, pride, habit, loneliness, whatever. Need wasn't always a good thing. Need wasn't something Aled had ever thought to be a sign of being loved.

But want?

Gabriel wanted to be here, dozing off on Aled's shoulder. He wanted to leave his dirty bike in the conservatory. He wanted to cook for two in the evenings. He wanted to hitch a ride in Aled's car, or on Aled's lap. He wanted telly evenings and pub dinners together.

He didn't need it. He could walk out whenever he liked. There was always somewhere else he could be, someone else he could be with. Aled was not — and had never been — his only option.

But he wanted to be here.

"I love you," Aled murmured.

But Gabriel was already asleep.

* * * *

Aled stepped out of work on Tuesday morning for an hour.

His office was in the middle of Leeds. The commute was shit, but his promotion into upper management had scored him a space in the underground car park. Normally, he'd never dream of going anywhere in the middle of the day. Traffic in the city centre just wasn't worth it.

But this time, his target didn't require a car. After all, the shopping centre was only minutes away. And — unlike in Wakefield — there was no chance he'd be seen in Leeds in the middle of the day and the news get back to his nosy partner.

He walked briskly, and the other shoppers skirted around him as he radiated a similar kind of deadly power to that he gave off in a game or a boardroom battle. Beggars didn't bother calling to this arrogant fuck in a Boxing Day sale suit. The charity workers aimed their false smiles somewhere else. A couple of young women — and one man — took a second glance for rather different reasons, but Aled ignored them. He had eyes only for the shimmering displays in the window of the shop at the end of the street.

A sea of silver was set out before him, draped over velvet clothes and silk cushions. Glittering gold framed the silver centre and other, richer, darker colours gleamed from within their chains and frames. Rubies. Pearls. Sapphires. The brilliant play of an opal in the afternoon sun. The pale authority of a fat diamond sitting arrogantly above the rest. Tiny labels, covered in beautifully neat copperplate handwriting, set out prices that ranged from easy to eye-watering. And the trinkets themselves had a similar range. From gaudy garnets to elegant emeralds, from the oversized to the understated, Aled could have bought a hideous screamer of new money for a loathed mother-in-law, or a shy statement of staggering wealth for his other woman.

But he didn't want any of those.

It took only a few moments to pick out the piece he'd see on their website. It was tucked away high in the window, almost totally obscured by other offerings with similar stones. Oddly common, strangely unique. Staggering beauty amidst a plain, almost cheap, setting. It had looked good online, and it looked even better there. He could see it elsewhere, too. See it framed by pale skin. See it where it *belonged.*

Aled blew out a breath and steeled himself, before reaching for the door and stepping into the cool interior of the jeweller's shop.

"Good afternoon, sir," twinkled a girl young enough to be his daughter. "Can I help you?"

"Yes," Aled said. "I want to buy something special."

Chapter Eighteen

Aled slammed the boot.

The big day was—well, days away. He had everything packed. Suze was calling almost every day with the latest drama, gripe, panic, moan, whine, *anything*. And yesterday had been his last day at work for ten days—and this morning, his last day at home until after his best friend was married.

God, it felt weird.

It was almost like going on another business trip. He had his sunglasses propped up on his hair, ready for several hours of driving straight at the sun. Two suits packed—the real deal and the just-in-case spare. He'd even had the car valeted so there'd not be any dust or muck that would get past the protective wrapping. And the fresh haircut still felt odd against the collar of his polo shirt.

Then there was Gabriel. Stood on the doorstep in his pyjamas and dressing gown like a 1960s housewife. All he was missing was the hair in rollers.

"Right," Aled said. "Need anything else before I go?"

"Yes," Gabriel said, standing in his slippers with his arms folded and a smirk on his face. "You to go."

Aled raised his eyebrows. "Tone like that, I might just shove you in the boot and take you with me."

"Not all of us can get that much time off work," Gabriel countered, then came down off the step for a kiss. "Anyway, I'm at work this afternoon, then Kevin's told me to go round this evening. And apparently I'm staying the night."

"Ooh, good luck with that," Aled quipped. He squeezed Gabriel's perfect bum, memorising it before Kevin tore it to shreds, then let go. "Okay, I better hit the road."

"Text me when you get there."

"Yup. Let me know what train you book so I can pick you up in St Ives."

"I'll stop off to see Chris on the way."

"Okay, but don't be late or Suze will send me to get you."

"Yeah, yeah."

Aled laughed as he threw himself in the car. Engine on, radio up, handbrake down, one last wave out of the open window and that was that. He peeled out into the street and set off south.

He'd used up the additional leave the firm had offered in the wake of his trip to the USA on going down to Cornwall early. Tom's dad was putting up the wedding party in the same fancy hotel hosting the entire affair and Aled wasn't going to say no to a free hotel room and Suze's company for a while on the Cornish coast. Even if he suspected he'd be thoroughly busy with keeping her from murdering her mother-in-law.

Spring had finally put some effort into it, the sun warming the car nicely as he wound his way out of Wakefield. Flowers were bobbing their heads on the side of the slip road as he surged down onto the motorway, then he put the price tag on the car to good use and floored it.

He was in a good mood and feeling arrogantly happy about his lot in life. Designer sunglasses. Car effortlessly soaring down the fast lane past chavs in Corsas, grandmas in ancient Golfs and lardy blokes in lorries. Good tunes on his favourite radio station. His penguin suit swaying from the hook in the back seat, professionally dry-cleaned and still in its wrapper, ready for his best friend's big day. A pleasant buzz from a goodbye blow job in the shower from his hotter-than-hell partner. What wasn't to like?

It was a long drive from Wakefield to St Ives, but Aled broke it up with a couple of stops, a picturesque detour down the Welsh side of the border then back across the Severn, and a pub lunch in Devon, hiding in the shade to protect himself from the cheery sun. Suze would never forgive him if he got sunburn in time for her photos. He took a few selfies of his own, taunting both her and Gabriel with his journey, and felt so sunny that even the heavy traffic of tourists heading for the Cornish coast couldn't upset him. Sheep in the road? Who cared. Roadworks? Necessary. Detour? All the more countryside to see. Nothing bothered him. Nothing mattered.

This was *life,* and Aled was loving it.

It was getting dark by the time he got to St Ives, the sky a stunning orange as he finally dropped down into the town. It worked in his favour. A small seaside town with a healthy supply of tourists, and Aled was going the opposite way to everyone else at dusk. It was busy enough to keep him paying attention, but not so busy that he felt pressured and anxious about not knowing his way. He'd never been before, but it looked nice enough. The sat nav knew its thing. And if Tom's dad's company owned a string of B&Bs and holiday cottages, then the hotel at St Ives was the jewel in their crown.

It didn't look much from the outside. Redbrick building. Offensively small car park. Lavender bushes brimming over with bees, humming happily in the warm spring air. He managed to squeeze into a free spot in the far corner and surveyed it with an unimpressed eye as he fetched his bits and bobs.

But the moment he walked through the doors, it was like stepping into another world.

Specifically, one where everyone lived in their own personal Ritz hotel.

The lobby was gleaming marble under a bright chandelier. The receptionist wore a waistcoat. Everything smelled of fresh flowers and fancy perfumes. There was a bellboy summoned to take his bags, even though there were only four floors to the whole building. And his room —

Well, okay, the room wasn't actually the most impressive one he'd ever seen — his firm used Hiltons when they sent their executive officers anywhere — but the minibar was generous and he had a nice view of the harbour. There was space. A deep carpet and mid-range art on the walls. He texted Gabriel a picture of the bed, took a quick shower to dust off a day's driving then collapsed into the pillows wearing just his towel. It was sinfully comfortable, and sleep beckoned, but he figured that he ought to do his duty first.

So he rang Suze.

"Ooh, hello! What's —"

"I'm here," Aled said.

"What?"

"I'm here. In St Ives."

She shrieked. He jerked the phone away, but far too late to save his eardrum.

"Oh my *God*! Tom! *Tom*! Aled's already here! Are you at the hotel? Have you had dinner? Come and have dinner with me." He heard something bang on her end and metal clinking. "We'll go and get fish and chips — there's a great place on the harbour — and I'll show you the house we've put an offer on."

Aled grinned. "Still naked here, Suze. Slow down."

"Then put clothes on, you stupid git!" A door banged. "You have ten minutes. Five. Whatever. What room number are you in?"

"Seven thousand, two hundred and two," he lied, still making no move to get up and get dressed.

"Be like that. Frank booked all the third floor for the wedding, so I'll just keep ringing you until I find you."

"It's called 'on silent.'"

"Stop being such a *slag*!"

He laughed and hung up on her, then switched his phone off to really hack her off. Then — because he had no doubt Suze would just knock on doors until she found him by process of elimination — he swung his legs down and headed for his bags to find some fresh underwear.

God, he was going to miss her once the wedding was over.

Seven minutes later, he heard footsteps and swearing in the hall. He shoved a polo shirt over his head before opening the door and was punched in the arm before getting his hug.

"Bastard."

"Guilty." He squeezed, swung her around, then shut the door. "Give me a second. Just need to get my wallet and a jumper."

"I like the new haircut!"

"Gabriel bitched like you wouldn't believe."

"When he's coming down?" she asked, collapsing onto the end of the bed while he fished a jumper out of the open bag.

"Night before. Be nice to have some peace and quiet."

"Liar."

"Yeah."

"What about Nana?"

"She doesn't think she'll be up to it."

"I'm not surprised," she said, though there was a wistful expression on her face. "I'll send her loads of pictures, though."

"Yeah, you better."

"Did you make up your mind in the end?" she asked, cocking her head.

"About what?"

"Proposing to Gabriel."

Aled rolled his eyes. "Right, where's these fish and chips, then?"

"Answer me!"

"No. Nosy cow."

"No, you won't answer me? No, you didn't decide? No, you won't?"

"I have decided, but I'm not going to answer you."

"Oh my God, that's a yes!"

"Lay off," he grumbled as she catapulted up to hug him again. "I'm not giving you any more information than that."

"That's *definitely* a yes," she said dreamily. "I get to be best woman."

"You're not the best woman at owt. Ow!"

"Deserved it. Twat."

She sulked all the way out to the car, then brightened up after Aled forked out for the fish and chips and she drove them up to the outskirts of the town with a car stinking of grease and vinegar. In a little cul-de-sac just before the town turned into countryside, she pulled over and pointed at a low, whitewashed cottage with a dark, thatched roof, sulking beyond an unkempt hedge and overshadowed by an enormous oak.

"We put in an offer last night," she said. "Three bedrooms. It's a little bit cramped downstairs but the garden is huge out to the back. And we only want a couple of kids anyway."

"Did Tom's parents say that before they had seventeen?"

"If you *ever* imply I have *anything* in common with Brenda again, I will *end* you."

Aled mimed zipping his lips.

"About kids…"

He eyed her, then—quite deliberately—eyed her stomach.

"Tom and I were talking names, but I wanted to run one by you first."

"Isn't names a bit premature? Or are they not, and that's the point you're getting at?"

"I'm not giving you any more information than that," she said loftily.

"Well, if your conclusion is I'm proposing, then mine is you're pregnant."

She stuck her chin in the air and repeated herself.

"Fine, fine. What's this name, then?"

"Euan."

Aled paused.

Plastic fork halfway to his mouth, he just stopped. For a beat, there was nothing. Then he slowly put it down and cleared his throat.

"Euan."

It sounded both familiar and foreign. He'd barely ever said it out loud, because why would he? There'd only been one Euan that Aled had ever known—and Aled had called him Dad.

Euan Evans. Soft Tenby accent. Terrible darts player. Keen cricketer. Had worn granddad jumpers since before he was even a dad. Used to build model ships, sitting hunched over the desk in the study with his glasses perched on the end of his nose and his tongue sticking out of the corner of his mouth as he tweaked a sail into place with a pair of tweezers. Aled still had that photo somewhere of Dad on the yacht, beaming after the sailing experience day that Mum had bought him for his fiftieth birthday.

He would have been only seventy-three now. She would have been only seventy. Another c-word, and one that Aled hated far more than the word cunt.

It was so stupid that it was over.

"I like it," he croaked.

His hand was warm. Suze's fingers were in his own. He blinked. A tear escaped, and she squeezed gently.

"He'd have been dead chuffed to be a granddad," he whispered.

"Yeah," Suze said. "He'd have been so good at it too."

"Well, he was a pretty decent dad."

"I don't know, he turned out *you* —"

"Hey!"

They laughed quietly in the dark bubble of the car, food forgotten. The shadow of loss retreated. Aled squeezed her hand in return and ducked his head to peer out at the cottage again.

"It'll be too small," he said. "I've seen you and babies before. It'll be five kids before you know it and you'll have to move again."

"Like hell I'm pushing out five kids."

"You say that now — "

"You can walk back to the hotel if that's your line," she threatened.

He grinned. "Idle threats."

"*Promises*."

"Whatever. What if you have a girl?"

"Oh, God. At least Tom's idea for a boy was okay. I had to totally veto his idea for a girl."

"What was it?"

"Naomi!"

"What's wrong with Naomi?"

"Erm, hello? Little Miss Universe from accounting? I don't think so!"

Aled agreed for the sake of keeping the peace. He honestly couldn't put a face to whoever it was in accounting who'd tarnished the name so badly.

"If we have girls, they'll be Amy and Isla and that's *it*. No Naomis!"

"That's only two options."

"There'll only be two kids!"

"*Suuuure…*"

Aled leaned his head back against the rest, smiling out at the lights from the nearby cottages. The *For Sale* sign creaked in the breeze. He could imagine it busier. Suze shrieking at her husband and twenty-five kids as they rampaged around. Tom being an even bigger kid than he was now. Weekends down on the Cornish coast, never having to assume responsibility for his nieces and nephews because he'd make Gabriel do it. Reminding said partner at every available opportunity about Aled's lack of fertility in case he went getting any ideas.

"Dad would have been proud of the both of us," he said.

Suze said nothing.

But she touched his wrist, and he turned his hand over to hold hers.

Chapter Nineteen

Gabriel had plans.

He didn't have any interest in being dragged to all sorts of last-minute wedding bollocks, and big family affairs were the stuff of nightmares whether they were his family or not—so Gabriel had no intention of wasting his time off on being bored shitless by Suze's mother-in-law.

But he had a few days beforehand to kill.

So he sent a text, bought a train ticket and put the bike back together from its maintenance in the muddy conservatory.

Chris didn't live in Bristol itself, but a small village south of it called Nailsea. It was a long journey to Bristol Temple Meads, then a walk over a pretty bridge in the Victorian station to a shuttle train that made the frumpy Queen Victoria herself look hip and modern. It was empty when he got on, set off late with no reason why and shuddered, banged, groaned, wailed and squealed its way south through grubby suburbs, over a filthy river and into the charming hills of north Somerset, brooding darkly under a sulking sky.

It wasn't quite what he'd imagined.

Nailsea stuck up out of the trees like a lost world. The only other passenger who had boarded at Bristol Temple Meads was sound asleep, and Gabriel stepped off alone onto a tiny slab of tarmac masquerading as a platform. The trainline was stuck up onto a manmade ridge above a background of fields and trees, houses nestled into the spare nooks and crannies. It was pretty, in an isolated sort of way. It screamed *crime thriller*. Maybe *Midsomer Murders* had a point.

With nobody there to meet him, and only one way out, Gabriel figured that it couldn't hurt to get down. God only knew what a fast train through here might do. He hefted his bike down a steep flight of hard stairs to the road, intending to wait and watch the world go by—but was immediately met by a short, stocky ex-soldier with a shaven head.

Gabriel grinned.

The ex-soldier smiled shyly back.

"Hey," Gabriel said. "So, your place or mine?"

The smile widened into a smirk. Chris pushed off from the wall he'd been lounging against as though there hadn't been a few hundred miles between them, and as though he hadn't been begging for Gabriel to come and visit for weeks. He just—smirked. Like they were old friends.

Gabriel's skin tingled, and he scolded himself for the reaction.

"C'mon."

There was no affection. Maybe it was too open for Chris' comfort. Maybe Nailsea was a nest of bigots. Maybe the sky was just too damn threatening. Gabriel didn't much care. There wouldn't be far to go in a tiny place like this. He sat on the bike and pushed it along with one foot idly, keeping a slow pace with Chris and not bothering with words until they turned into a street of shops and Chris fished keys from his pocket.

"C'mon," he mumbled. "Erm. Hopefully Jack's gone to work."

The keys belonged to a metal fire escape that rose out of an alley of dustbins, wedged between a Chinese takeaway and a presumably competing fish and chip shop. They wrestled the bike up the stairs between them, and Gabriel admired the industrial chic style as Chris picked another key and had to bodyslam the wooden door to unstick it from the frame.

"Oh," he said.

Jack hadn't gone out. The wooden door popped open into a kitchen and they immediately ran into a blond bloke in his mid-twenties shovelling cereal down his neck and fighting his way into a hi-vis vest. The kitchen was a reasonable size but looked like a student flat. A bottle of green milk—not green top, but *green*—was festering in the sink. Dirty plates were stacked up in the window. The tiles were all different colours, though it didn't look deliberate, and the wallpaper made the décor reminiscent of Aled's nana's flat before she'd moved into the care home.

Gabriel bit back a smirk and propped his bike up in a clean—ish—corner.

"Hey, man," Jack said, chewing noisily. "We're out of milk. Can you get some later? Oh, and Jim called about the rent. Can you make up mine this month? Cool. I gotta run. Hey, Chris' girlfriend."

"Boyfriend," Gabriel said automatically.

"Hey, Chris' boyfriend."

Then the orange vest shot past the bike, bowl still in hand, and the stairs were thumping and rattling like they'd come away from the wall. Gabriel smothered a laugh as Chris slammed the door and shot him a smirk.

"Roommate?"

"Yeah." Chris was a little pink. "Sorry about that. Um. And, you know. The state of this place."

"S'fine."

"I asked him to clean up his shit, but...yeah."

"Hey, I said it's fine. Not like I'm trying today." Gabriel stepped closer and looped his arms around Chris' neck. "So, you want to say hello, or you just going to grunt at me like a big dumb lout?"

Chris laughed. He ducked his head to do it, like he was shy. Gabriel's heart clenched and something fluttered low in his stomach. Chris had dimples when he smiled, and they were...cute.

On a whim, Gabriel darted in for a kiss, and the laugh was snuffed out. A hand settled in the small of his back. Lips sought his like they were as shy as their owner, and Gabriel coaxed Chris out from behind his armour. He had no hair to play with, but maybe that was for the best. Gabriel could concentrate that way. Chase the taste of him. Push and push and push, until they were backed into the fridge and both of Chris' hands were mapping out every dip and curve of Gabriel's back.

Then Chris broke it to nuzzle at Gabriel's neck and breathe in as though Gabriel were *life*.

"Hello," he whispered.

"Hello."

"Missed you."

Gabriel pulled back, dragging their joined hands out between them until they slipped apart.

"Me too," he admitted gently, then grinned. "Wanna show me how much?"

"I was thinking…takeaway and TV in my room?" Chris offered. "Jack will be out all evening, so —"

"Sounds like it's time get comfortable, then." Gabriel cocked his head, grinning. "Wanna help me out of this bra?"

The flat might have been grubby, but it was warm. And fighting the bike up the stairs — well, Gabriel wanted a shower. Maybe with company, maybe without. He turned his back and shucked his T-shirt. For a brief second, warm fingers traced up his spine then fell away.

"I'm — I'm good, thanks."

Gabriel chewed on the corner of his lip, then turned around. Chris' eyes flickered down, then darted away again. Gabriel hesitated then reached out to clasp Chris' wrist. Maybe it was time to chip away at the little wall that had gone up in Chris' head.

"You wanna try thinking those thoughts out loud?"

Chris clenched his jaw and shook his head.

"Why not?" Gabriel prompted gently.

Chris huffed. "I don't understand them. You won't. They'll — They're not good. And — and I want this weekend to be good."

"Try me."

"You wouldn't understand."

"Try me anyway," Gabriel said. "Or maybe I could do some thinking out loud and you could tell me if I'm way off base?"

Chris' gaze stayed riveted to the floor. Slowly, Gabriel reached out to take the other wrist and slid a little closer.

"I don't think you like sex."

Chris flinched. Gabriel held on.

"I think sometimes you need it, but you don't actually like it. I don't think you want to sleep with me, but if you do, it means you can go longer than if you just jerk off. But I think you still want to go out with me, and maybe that's confusing too. Because you want me, but you don't *want* me."

Chris wriggled his forearms. His wrists slid through Gabriel's grip, but then his fingers caught and curled about Gabriel's own.

"I—"

But that was it. He coughed and stopped again, shaking his head. Gabriel nudged a little closer, until the lace of his bra faintly touched Chris' T-shirt.

"It's okay."

"Is it?"

Chris' voice cracked in the middle, and Gabriel squeezed.

"Yes."

"It's not."

"Sure it is," Gabriel whispered. "I like you for more than just your dick, you know?"

A tiny laugh bubbled up—then the bubbles burst and Chris' face crumpled. Gabriel let go of his hands just to catch the back of his neck and draw him in. The tears were hot on Gabriel's skin.

"It's okay," Gabriel repeated. "It really is, I promise. I didn't catch a train today because I like your dick or the way you fuck me. I caught it because I like the face you pull at fantasy movies and the smirk you give me when you win our cycling races. I wanted to see Somerset with you from our bikes and talk you into tossing that stupid diet and having a doughnut with me from Greggs. I wanted to see *you*. I can have penis up north, you know, it's not *that* backward. I don't need a train for that."

The strange mixture of crying, hiccupping and laughing rocked into his shoulder and Gabriel grinned, squeezing tight and warming to his theme.

"You make me feel warm," he continued. "You give me that funny little swoop in my chest sometimes. Aled says he knows when you've texted me kisses because I make a dumb face. And I want that more than I want to have sex with you. I can have fantastic sex from any guy who can rock a cock, but there's only a couple of people can make me feel like that. And one's right here."

"*Why.*"

It was a harsh demand, and Gabriel rolled his eyes.

"Fuck, I don't know. It's just like that, I guess. I don't know why I fell in love with Aled either. I'm just…there. I am. Like I am with you."

It had taken a long time to admit it with Aled and Gabriel smiled into the top of Chris' shoulder as he realised what Aled had bloody well done. Domesticated him. The utter bastard. There was a time when Gabriel would have balked at the idea of being in love. He wouldn't have wanted to feel it and he'd have been scared of what it meant. He'd taken so damn long to admit what he felt for Aled — and now here he was, throwing it out like nobody's business.

"S'not normal," Chris croaked eventually.

"Bugger normal."

"No thanks."

Gabriel snorted with laughter. Arms locked around his waist and he rocked gently on his hips, swaying them idly side to side as Chris burrowed into him.

"What's not normal?" he prompted.

"Not—not liking it."

So he was right.

"It's probably not normal to get off on pretending to be raped," Gabriel said gently. "It's kind of weird to enjoy being beaten by your boyfriend. And you know what I found out the other day? Greg's got a thing for *feet*. That's just—*ew*. Feet are gross."

"Feet are pretty," Chris mumbled.

"Says who? Hobbits? Feet are gross. All verrucas and hard dead bits and *toe hair*. Fucking *toe hair*. What's pretty about that, you freak?"

It worked like a charm. Chris broke away with a barking laugh, shaking his head, and Gabriel followed, seizing him by the ears and demanding to know what dirty secrets he had.

"Next you'll be saying ankles are sexy! Bones jutting out isn't *sexy*, oh my God!"

He chased Chris through the little flat—the grubby kitchen and the threadbare living room, past a still-steaming bathroom and into a messy bedroom with paint peeling off the walls and a cute framed photo on the bookshelf, of the pair of them on the Trans Pennine Trail the first week after Aled had gone to America. They flopped down into the narrow bed and Gabriel inched over until he was lying across Chris' arm. He pressed a light kiss to his shoulder, then took his hand and placed it lightly against his right breast.

"Do you like touching it?"

Chris swallowed.

"It's okay if you don't," Gabriel murmured. "I'm not going to get mad."

"I—"

For a split second, Chris' fingers spread. Gabriel didn't have large boobs, and it was almost completely covered by Chris' palm, disappearing entirely under his fingers. then the hand slid sideways, coming to rest in the dip between hip and shoulder.

"No."

"Okay," Gabriel said, squeezing his wrist. "What does it feel like?"

Chris licked his lips.

"I feel—"

Gabriel waited, stroking the fine hairs on his arm lightly.

"I want to pull away," Chris whispered eventually.

"Repulsed?"

Chris flinched again. "You're not—"

"S'not about me," Gabriel said.

"But it is. I l—like you. I should—"

"I knew this guy once who'd puke about body fluids. Ironically," he added tartly. "He *had* to wear a rubber, and I had to take it off when we were done. We used to play doctors because if he fingered me, he had to wear a glove."

"Seriously?" Chris' expression was suspicious. "You're making that up."

"Swear on my life," Gabriel said. He smirked. "If I was mad at him, I'd deliberately sneak off to the bathroom beforehand to jerk off so I was so wet he'd feel it anyway."

Chris raised a single eyebrow.

"Really, being turned off by a boob isn't *that* unusual."

"S'not just the boob though, is it?"

"What else is it?"

"Everything."

"My waist?"

The hand lying on said waist flattened out a little.

"No," Chris said. "But that's not —"

"Do you like to hold my hand? To hug me? To kiss me?"

Gabriel already knew the answers to those and knocked his knuckles against Chris' breastbone when he nodded.

"Doesn't sound like everything."

"Everything sexual, then."

"That's not very much in the grand scheme of things," Gabriel replied.

"I guess…"

"So why did we have sex those other couple of times?"

Chris grimaced. "I — nothing's wrong with my dick."

"It gets hard and you gotta go?"

"Yeah."

"Is that what happened? You were hard and I was there?"

"Guess so."

"Did you like it?"

Chris mutely shook his head. He looked utterly miserable and Gabriel nudged his nose against the tip of Chris' before carrying on.

"Why not ignore it?"

"I need to," Chris croaked hoarsely. "It's — like — I get sexually frustrated sometimes. And when we did it, it lasted way longer before I needed to do it again than if I just jacked it. I just — I don't — I hate it. The throbbing and the heat and it leaks and —"

Gabriel made a soothing noise, rapping his sternum again when Chris' voice started to roll into a panicked babble.

"You reckon it's going to happen while I'm here?"

"Probably."

"So why don't we try something?" he suggested softly. "If it happens, let me deal with it. I think I know something that might help."

"What's that?"

Gabriel nudged their noses together, waiting for the tension in Chris' shoulders to ease before he started whispering.

"Let me take care of everything."

"What do you mean?"

"You don't touch," Gabriel murmured. "You don't look. You keep your eyes on mine, and I will do everything so you don't have to. I'll get you off, nice and easy, and you won't have to see it or smell it or go through the motions if you don't want to."

It wouldn't be the first time Gabriel had had to do all the work, but it would be the first time it wasn't a game. Chris could get hard on his own — Gabriel already knew that from experience — but if he didn't want to touch anything, then he didn't have to.

"I can only take off what I have to. I'm not going to be exactly upset if you don't want to get involved with all my curves. It'll be drier if we use a condom. We can play music or a film, or you can just talk to me if you've got the skills to do it."

Chris huffed a weak laugh. "Seriously? Skills?"

"Hey, a lot of guys can't. *I* usually can't."

"That's weak."

Gabriel bit back a laugh. That was...yeah, he was increasingly sure that Chris had an asexual streak. A *wide* one.

"It doesn't have to be anything more than a bit of sitting in your lap and a nice warm grip. That's it."

"You'd — you'd do that?"

"Hey, I like the feeling of something inside me just as much as the actual sex part. And I have other guys to drill me." Gabriel pressed his smile against Chris' cheek for a brief moment before backing off again. "I like you. Not your dick. And at risk of upsetting your male ego, it's not the most magnificent dick in the world, so you shouldn't be *that* surprised."

The trick worked. He earned another little chuckle.

"You need me to help out sometimes so you don't feel bad," Gabriel whispered. "Don't you think I of all people know what that feels like?"

He let the question hang in the air. For a brief moment, Chris' gaze dropped. They hadn't talked about it, not since Gabriel had first told him that he wasn't the girl Chris had assumed him to be at first sight. Chris had just said, "Oh," then asked him on a date anyway. And okay, Gabriel had avoided the subject because he hadn't wanted to be Chris' gay/straight experiment, but—

This wasn't what he'd thought.

This was a sexual-or-not experiment, and that was nothing to do with anybody's bits.

"I might be a sex fiend, but I know how to make it so it's about as sexy as waiting in line for a bus, too," Gabriel said. "Next time you need to and I'm around, let me try that. It might help."

"And—"

He knew what was coming next.

"If it doesn't," he murmured, "then we just try something else until we figure out what fits."

Chris bit his lip. His hand slid up Gabriel's side, skirting around his tits like they were on fire, before sliding into his hair and slowly teasing it up into its usual unruly spikes.

"Why are you like this?" he asked.

"Huh?"

"Chill. I'm bust. What guy doesn't like to fuck? And you're just—chill."

Gabriel laughed. He pushed himself up, shoving Chris over onto his back and straddling his waist. For a split second, Chris tensed—then relaxed as Gabriel flopped into him and nestled his head into the juncture of Chris' neck and shoulder.

"I like stuff that most people would call totally crazy," he said. "I don't even have to get off sometimes and I still liked the fuck. A man who doesn't like sex isn't that weird."

"Keep telling yourself that," Chris mumbled.

"I will. 'Cause it's true. You know what else is totally crazy? Guys with vaginas—oh, wait."

Chris laughed, and it felt real. It rocked up out of his chest and disturbed Gabriel's boneless slump. He complained and Chris rolled him off the bed entirely— before sitting up and smiling gently down at him.

"Thanks," he said.

"No problem," Gabriel replied, and reached up to squeeze his knee. "I love you. If you're asexual or whatever, then…still love you."

Chris gripped his wrist and squeezed back.

"Asexual," he echoed.

Gabriel didn't think that it was a question.

Chapter Twenty

Penzance train station was surprisingly busy.

The sky was turning orange as the sun sank towards the horizon. Aled lounged against the wall as the northbound train left again and the bubble of passengers slowed to a trickle. Originally the plan had been that Gabriel simply jumped on the connecting service to St Ives, but Suze's bellowed argument with her future mother-in-law had put paid to that idea. So here Aled was, pushing himself forward and opening his arms for a hug as Gabriel came bouncing in from the platform.

"Good weekend with Chris?"

"Yep. How's wedding planning going?"

"Kill me," Aled deadpanned. "I was less stressed about my own damn wedding and we had to get it done and dusted before Dad passed away."

"Christ, that bad?"

"If there's not a murder by the big day, I'll be impressed."

Gabriel whistled lowly as they paced out to the car. It had been an intensely hot day, and twilight had done very little to alleviate it. The dying light ricocheted off Gabriel's black hair until it turned an inky blue. His skin glowed like marble and Aled rolled his eyes as the aviator glasses were fished out of a pocket and slid into place. And — of course — heads started to turn.

"Slag," he muttered.

"And proud. So what's happened to make shit hit the fan?"

"Tom's mum thinks Suze is pregnant."

"So?"

Aled smirked. "Somehow she had it in her head that her lovely boys only married virgins."

Gabriel snorted. "One of her lovely boys brought his boyfriend to my flat and they took turns fucking me to see how much cum I can hold before I start leaking."

"What, once each?"

"Lying fucktard."

Aled dodged the blow and laughed. He beat a hasty retreat to the driver's seat but was smacked anyway when Gabriel got into the car.

"So Mrs Hooper's from the dark ages, then?"

Aled shrugged as he turned the key and the engine fired up. The air conditioning was in fine form, and he cranked it up before carefully easing the car back out of the space.

"*Is* Suze pregnant?"

"Dunno. Probably."

Gabriel grinned and called it exciting. Aled pulled a face and grumbled about being too young to be an uncle, his focus more on negotiating his way out of Penzance without killing an old lady or twatting a campervan than Suze's reproductive status.

"Well, I'm not Cornish," Gabriel said once Penzance fell away and they were ripping through the countryside, the sea shimmering on the left and open fields glowing on the right, "but this isn't the way to St Ives."

"Nope."

"Where are we going, then?"

Aled had planned just a long pub dinner and a long drive home, so the hotel would be quiet and both Brenda and Suze in their respective beds before they got back. But—

Gabriel was lounging in the passenger seat, all long limbs and loose cotton. He was dressed in a pair of trainers, a baggy tank top, a pair of board shorts and nothing else. No socks. No binder. No bra. The faint loop of his nipple ring was barely there against the fall of his top, and when he lifted his arm to point at a bird of prey wheeling out over the Channel, the faintest shadow of a curve could be seen beyond his armpit. His slim legs had darkened from their usual marble white after doing whatever he'd been doing with Chris all weekend. There were freckles dancing under his sunglasses, and in the creases of his smile. He looked lax and pliant. An odd mixture of alluring and innocent.

Aled wanted him.

"Beach."

"Why?"

Because Aled knew a cove with hidden corners not far from Penzance. Because the sun was going down. Because the tide was still out. Because there'd be nobody there now. Because Gabriel was in high spirits, basking in the dusk as they slipped along the slowly darkening coast, and Aled couldn't decide whether to add fuel to the fire or whether to snuff out the spark.

Sure enough, the little car park had only one other car left, with exhausted parents already wrestling their offspring into the back seats. The beach itself was a ten-minute walk through still-warm countryside, and they reached the top of the cove just as the sun slipped beneath the lip of the horizon, and the sky turned a pale blue above an ink-black sea. The scramble down the rocks was aided by the torch on Aled's phone, then he slipped it away once their shoes hit sand and caught the button of Gabriel's shorts between finger and thumb.

"Strip," he said.

Gabriel stripped without a word. His clothes simply fell to the sand in a crumpled puddle and he stood silently in the centre of them, eyes downcast. Obedient. Submissive. Aled worked his jaw, then nodded to the water.

"Get in."

Gabriel's foot shifted slightly in the sand.

"And don't turn your back on your owner."

The foot twisted and Gabriel carefully stepped into the water. It was cold. The hairs on Gabriel's arms fluffed up in a matter of seconds and he bit his lip when Aled ordered him to kneel, then keep going.

When the first idle wave swamped his face, Aled told him to stop.

Then he stripped from the waist down and followed him. Stopping with his soft cock just an inch from Gabriel's mouth, he ran a hand through wet hair and pulled until those large dark eyes stared up at him.

"The tide's coming in," he said, "and you don't get out until the job's done. So I'd get a move on if I were you."

The water was like ice, but Gabriel's mouth and hands were hot. And the coughing and gagging as he choked on dick and seawater was even hotter. Aled sighed as his balls were massaged in warm hands and his cock worked like a musical instrument. And Gabriel was playing the fastest solo known to man. The rhythm was almost hard, the pass of lips up and down the shaft so quick that it almost chafed. Once, Aled idly reached down to grab Gabriel's hair and force the head into his throat, and the thrash and gag had an edge of panic that was both dangerous and alluring.

He would drown if he didn't hurry up, and he knew it.

And Aled had just intended on getting a blow job and heading back to the car for a proper fuck, where they would be tangled up in the too-small space and Gabriel would be utterly defenceless against whatever Aled wanted to do, but the added layer of vulnerability was just too tempting. He yanked that damp face off his dick just before the point of no return and for a split second, Gabriel slipped entirely beneath the waves.

And when he emerged, coughing and shivering, Aled seized a fistful of hair, and shook him.

"Move."

He bullied him up the shore until they stood knee-deep, then took hold of his hips and brushed his cock up against a tight, unprepared arse.

"Your choice," he whispered. "A spit-fuck in the back, or a salted one in the front."

Either would be uncomfortable. Possibly even hurt, if Gabriel hadn't had any sex with Chris during his stay in Bristol. But pain was second only to humiliation when it came to getting Gabriel's rocks off, and Aled wasn't too surprised when Gabriel whispered, "Th-the back," through chattering teeth.

"Put your hands on the sand."

"What?"

He slapped that captured arse as hard as he could and Gabriel stumbled.

"Get up!"

Gabriel staggered back to his feet, then did as he'd been told and bent at the waist to plant his palms flat on the shore. It brought his face perilously close to the waves, and that had been the idea. As Aled slowly drove his cock into that tight, resisting arse, the whisper of pain was cut off by harsh spluttering against the incoming tide.

And with every cough, Gabriel *squeezed*.

It was like fucking a clenched fist. It was almost like fucking a virgin again and Aled relished the pressure. Pressure was one of the best damn things about getting his dick in someone. He liked the soft, wet grasp of a cunt around his fingers. He loved the taste of both kinds of lips on his tongue. But there was something utterly glorious about having his dick squeezed by a seemingly unwilling body as he fucked it anyway — and Aled *fucked* it. Fucked like his life depended on it. Fucked like Gabriel was a toy. Just held those hips in a vice-like grip and slammed in and out, in and out, in and out, until there was a grey blurring around the cliffs in the corner of his vision and the sea was warm around his feet.

When he came, he stayed right there for a long, long minute.

"Fuck," he breathed.

Eyes closed, he could feel the world shivering around the hammering of his own heart. He could feel every muscle in his entire body. He could feel the relaxed contentment in his cock, but also the urge to try again already building in his balls.

He pushed.

Gabriel vanished into the waves and lay crumpled before him, a pale shape in the growing dark. Aled left him there, walking back up to their clothes and shoving his wet feet into trousers and shoes, before gathering Gabriel's things under one arm and walking back down to him.

"Get up."

"J-just a—"

He caught Gabriel's hair and yanked it. Gabriel gasped, fumbling to his knees.

"You want another one?"

"No! No, sir!"

"You *don't* want my cock?"

"I—but—I—"

"Was I holding you down out there? Did I rip your clothes off? Did I drag you into the water? Did I?"

"N-no—"

"So you went out there because you wanted to."

Gabriel's mouth worked soundlessly.

"You went out there and got on your knees and sucked my cock because you wanted to. Then you bent over and asked me to fuck your arse. Isn't that right?"

"Y-yes, sir..."

"So what was that about my cock?"

"I—I want it, sir. I want it."

"You don't sound convinced."

"I do! I do, I—"

Aled let go. "Prove it. Back to the car. On your hands and knees."

Perhaps wisely, Gabriel didn't say anything or ask for his clothes back. He just set off crawling up the beach. Aled found his phone and put the torch back on and watched in no small amount of appreciation as he followed sedately behind. Ten minutes turned into twenty and the moon was high before Gabriel — scratched, bruised and shivering — reached the car. Aled made him wait on his knees in the gravel while he put the spare blanket down across the back seat, then threw his clothes in the boot and slammed it.

"Get in."

Gabriel crawled up onto the blanket and turned over to lie on his back. Aled smirked and crawled in after him. Over him. His warmth in his clothes against Gabriel's blue-tinged nudity. His bulk trapping that slim form under him. The child locks on the doors forming a prison, and the only key in Aled's possession.

"Now, how about you try again with those comments about my cock?"

Because his cock was hard again. Pressing against the zip on his jeans. Pressing against Gabriel's thighs — then not, as they slowly parted and Aled's hips slid into the space between them.

"I want you to fuck me," Gabriel whispered hoarsely. "I want you to fuck me like I'm nothing more like a warm hole. I want to feel your cock all the way ins — oh *God*, inside of me — "

The speech creaked around the edges as Aled unzipped his jeans and began to fuck him, a mixture of arousal and seawater sliding out around his dick with every push, but the words themselves never quite vanished.

" — to use me however — *fuck* — however you want — "

He allowed a tiny scrap of warmer emotion to enter the scene, in the form of a single kiss behind Gabriel's ear, then pulled the mantle of sadistic dominance back around himself, and bit.

After all, Gabriel hadn't come yet.

And after Aled had warmed him up, maybe he ought to beg for that, too.

Chapter Twenty-One

Gabriel woke up alone.

Judging by the light and the feeling of a long, intense sleep, it was early afternoon. He blinked sleepily around a small hotel room, comfortable bed undermined somewhat by the grubby wallpaper and the view of a brick wall out of the tiny window. The door was secured with a thin chain and a rusty bolt. The fire safety poster was yellow and peeling. He could hear the deep rattle of old pipes and a thin layer of steam was emerging from underneath the only other door in the room. He was well and truly shut away.

And when he threw back the covers, there was an ankle cuff and a short chain securing him to the bedframe.

"Aled?"

The rattling stopped.

"Game over, please!"

Something swished. The closer door opened and steam flooded out—along with a soaking wet partner, only a paper-thin towel around his waist hiding the cock that had fucked him into a coma last night.

Gabriel lifted his foot and wiggled it. "Red."

"Okay."

The key was produced. When the cuff popped over, Gabriel drew back his foot and crawled down the bed for a wet kiss. He nuzzled into Aled's damp embrace, inhaling deeply by his ear to catch the raw smell of him fresh out of the shower, then sat back on his heels with a grin.

"Feed me."

Aled laughed, cupped his face in both hands and kissed him again.

"Let me get dressed and we'll head back over to St Ives via a greasy spoon or something."

"This isn't St Ives?"

"Nope. Didn't fancy smuggling you into Tom's dad's fancy hotel after our game."

"Who's this 'our'?" Gabriel quipped, staggering off the bed. "*You* mindfucked me then *fuck*-fucked me."

"And you loved it."

"Besides the point."

Aled swatted his sore backside and Gabriel shot into the bathroom with an affronted scowl over his shoulder.

But at least the shower was good.

He felt more human afterwards, the hot water drumming out the memory of an icy sea, a brutal spit-fuck and a hell of a mindgame. His arms and legs were covered in light scratches and his knees looked like he'd knelt on a tennis court and sucked off every man in Wimbledon, but there was a contented buzz humming through his veins.

There was no way that he'd be saying red all day.

Aled was in a good mood too, twirling Gabriel like a dancer more than once as they got ready and talking more than he usually did in a week on their way to find breakfast. They were still near Penzance, so Gabriel put up a fight for a second breakfast once they got to St Ives and managed to even persuade Aled into a bit of a cuddle in the line at the bakery, despite Gabriel's near-beard and baggy T-shirt putting them at the mercy of the local bigots. Not that the old git with his fat Jack Russell on the harbourfront was much of a threat.

"You're a fucking nightmare," Aled told him through a post-pasty kiss. "Come on. I've got to go to the wedding rehearsal this afternoon and you need to get your suit unpacked so it won't crease."

"Squeeze my arse and I'll let go," Gabriel whispered in his ear.

"Fucking hell—"

"You can fuck me too, if you like."

"I *did*!"

"So?"

Aled sighed gustily but pinched his arse. Hard. Gabriel yelped and darted out of reach in case it wasn't a singular offence.

"That's what you get for toying with me," Aled said, and jerked his head towards the car park. "Come on."

Gabriel had been expecting a country-cottage-style thing. Old bar downstairs and cosy rooms upstairs. Not—

Well, not the fancy joint that Aled led him into.

The hotel was *posh*.

The gleaming lobby like an American bank, the classical music playing in the lift, the lush carpet in the halls. And the *room*. The en suite was the same size as Aled's bathroom back home, and when Gabriel perched on the edge of the bed, he sank about a foot into the mattress.

"Oh my God," he said. "This is insane."

Aled smirked, sitting on the edge of the bed and toeing his shoes off.

"Have you been staying here the whole time?"

"Yep."

"Fucking hell," Gabriel said. "I need a best friend with a super-rich boyfriend."

"You have a wealthy enough owner, don't get ahead of yourself," Aled said. He stood up and stretched. "Do you want to come to the rehearsal?"

"Not really," Gabriel admitted, watching the show as Aled steadily stripped out of his clothes. "Suze will need all your attention anyway. She's starting to panic, from what you said."

"That's not panic, that's trying not to murder her future mother-in-law," Aled quipped.

Gabriel chuckled, and forced himself out of the bed. "I'm going for another shower. If the last place was good, then I want to try this one."

"Okay. Let me have a slash first."

Gabriel stripped off at the bed and gave Aled a little naked dance as they swapped back again, then locked him out with a laugh. The bathroom was palatial. The shower was a tower of different heads and he was blasted with hot water from every angle until his skin ached. He washed every inch of himself and even lingered long enough for a wank before getting out and drowning himself in the enormous towels. He used up two before draping them back over the rails to dry and walking back out into the room.

And stopping dead.

Aled was—

"Oh my God."

In a dark grey suit, his hair perfectly slicked back and his glasses framing an intense blue stare, Aled looked like — like —

"*There* you are."

Gabriel's blood headed south. Rapidly. The drawling sneer. The folded arms over a chest pushing at the confines of a pristine waistcoat and sharp tie. The well-fitted trousers. The hard, cold look of a dominant with a brand-new game.

Gabriel's throat dried.

"Hurry up," Aled said, and snapped his fingers. He gestured to his feet. "On your knees."

"W-what?" Gabriel stammered.

"For fuck's sake," Aled sighed heavily. "*Get on your knees*. Is that difficult to understand?"

Gabriel hugged the towel around himself. His heart was beating wildly and the wet heat in his groin was nothing to do with the shower. Oh Christ. Aled was going to fuckface him looking like *that*? Like a lawyer and a client? Like a CEO and a secretary? Like a stockbroker and a whore?

Gabriel hadn't even known he had a thing for suits.

"I don't have time for this," Aled snapped and his hand lashed out. He seized Gabriel's wrist. Gabriel yelped and dropped the towel. But he wasn't driven to his knees. He was smashed down onto the end of the bed instead, face down in the duvet and hips hanging over the edge. A sharp dress shoe slapped at his ankle and kicked his legs apart and the sound of a zip was loud in the room.

"Don't — "

A hand shoved Gabriel's face down into the sheets.

"Shut up. What the hell did you think you were here for?"

Gabriel whined, shoving his hips up into Aled's groin even as he clawed at the sheets. God, he didn't even know he liked being fucked by arrogant pricks in suits. The porn was never that good and he'd never shagged anyone who'd tried it, but *fuck*. Fuck, he wanted it. *Now!*

It hurt.

He yowled into the sheets as Aled rammed his cock inside. He didn't pause, either. In a moment, Gabriel had gone from empty and over-sensitive from his wank in the shower to being ploughed like a field by a rock-hard dick. It was like being punched, over and over and over again. And it wasn't deep enough. Wasn't hard enough. He twisted and squirmed. He braced himself against the bed and tried to push back. Tried to rut on the sheets. Tried to resist.

"Fuck's sake, shut up!"

That hand shoved his head back down. Another landed between his shoulder blades, pressing him down into the mattress until he wheezed. The angle changed. It stabbed and dragged inside him, and the first sparks of erotic danger began to build in his crotch.

"What did you think I brought you here for, eh?" Aled grunted above him. "What, some nice weekend retreat? Candlelit dinners and a walk on the beach? Fuck off. This is what you're here for and you're done when I'm done."

The bed was rocking. The mattress groaned. Gabriel could only gasp wordlessly as he was ridden. There was nothing but the rhythm. The hot cock breaking him in half. The hand on his back, forcing him down. The sheets in his mouth, choking him—

A fist seized his hair and wrenched his head back. His jaw sagged open. One sharp, snapping thrust bowed him as though he'd break in half and the rush of cum was like being burned from the inside out. The slippery rush of Aled pulling out left him hollow and cold, and the weight on his back increased for a moment as Aled leaned down, his full weight driving Gabriel deeper into the suffocating bed.

"Should have done as you were told."

Tape ripped. Gabriel squirmed uselessly as his hands were bent up behind his back and taped securely together. Bound, he was turned over and each ankle taped to a bedpost, leaving him spread-eagled and face up on the bed.

Then Aled yanked a length of the dark tape out, and smirked.

"Very pretty."

The hotel room vanished and Gabriel shivered as more and more tape was added. The gloom turned to darkness, turned to blindness. Cold air drifted over him and he sensed Aled step away from the bed.

"You'll ruin the bed, leaking like that."

Gabriel tensed.

"*No!*"

"Shut up or I'll fucking gag you."

"*No-no-no-no—!*"

There was no give in the tape, in the bedposts, in Gabriel's legs. He was utterly trapped against the hard, cold plastic that pressed up against his used and abused cunt—then kept pressing. The dildo sank into him and a hand sealed his mouth as he howled. It *hurt*. It was *huge*. It just kept coming and coming, stretching him out until he swore he could hear the groan in his skin and hips. It pressed up into his stomach and guts like a baseball bat. When the base finally touched his labia, he gulped a heaving breath and swore that he could have vomited it up through his stomach.

He shuddered when the loops of metal closed over his hips.

"Much better."

The lock of the chastity belt was like the closing of a tomb. He couldn't push it out. He couldn't bend around it. There was nowhere to go, no way to escape — and with the tape securing him to the bed, no protection for when Aled decided to use him again.

"That should keep you busy until I get back."

The kiss was cruel and cold, but the next word soft against his ear.

"Colour?"

Gabriel gulped another heaving breath. He knew what came next. He'd be abandoned like this. Probably gagged. Blind and imprisoned and pinned on this massive, massive prick. The hours would feel like years. His cock would be permanently swollen. He'd itch to come. Then when Aled came back —

He'd rip it out, and fuck Gabriel until he screamed. Until he begged for it. Until he was black and blue and bleeding, and still begging for more. Until he'd come five, ten, fifteen times — then he'd be fucked all over again for daring to come before his master.

"Green."

A tiny, gentle touch against his chin. A soft kiss.

And the tape sealed his lips and he was abandoned, defenceless, in an empty hotel room.

* * * *

The door clicked.

Gabriel didn't know if he'd slept or not. He jumped when fingers touched his chin and the tape was peeled away. He waited for the kiss — or the cock — but neither came. Instead, Aled spoke. Gently. Not the harsh rasp of a dominant playing a game, but simply *Aled*.

"Pausing the game for a second, sweetheart. Understand?"

Gabriel nodded.

"I ran into Tom's brother at the rehearsal. Darren. Do you remember Darren?"

Gabriel nodded again. Small-world syndrome. Darren and his boyfriend had hooked up with Gabriel when they'd been visiting Yorkshire, years ago and before Gabriel had met Aled. Hell, they were *why* he'd met Aled. They'd recommended him when Aled had been looking for a fuck to get his soon-to-be ex-wife out of his system.

"He remembers you. Said he'd like to get acquainted again. And you did mention threesomes the other day."

Gabriel sucked in a breath. His mind raced. It was perfect. He trusted Daz. He'd been funny and sweet and respectful. He wasn't some scary stranger in a club. If it didn't work, he'd be okay with stopping. And if it did —

God, if it *did*.

"What do you want to do?"

"Do it," Gabriel whispered.

"How?"

"Anonymous."

Obviously it wouldn't be. But there could be some of it.

"Blindfolded. And my hands tied."

"Daz played with you like that before?"

Gabriel shook his head.

"Okay. I'll be here the whole time, though, so if you need out, you know what to do."

Gabriel nodded. He lay still as Aled unlocked the belt and carefully withdrew the punishing dildo. His legs were released and he folded himself up to sit on the pillows. Aled massaged his ankles lightly and nudged a gentle kiss against Gabriel's mouth.

"Say it for me."

"I want to be blindfolded and my hands tied and you and Daz fuck me together."

"How?"

"No mouth."

He wanted to shout. He wanted to feel two real dicks inside him, not rubber and silicone, and he wanted to feel them almost against each other too. He wanted heartbeats and pre-cum and the real fucking deal.

"No condoms."

Aled grunted. "We'll see about that part."

"He gets tested reg—"

"He did years ago. We'll see."

Gabriel gave up on persuading him about that. "Remind him about alcohol. I was sober by then, but he might not remember."

"All right."

"And I don't care who uses what. I don't want to know. I want to be confused."

"Sure?"

"Yeah."

Another kiss. Gabriel grinned around it and Aled laughed.

"Madman. Okay. I'll go talk to him. Don't go anywhere."

"How can I? You've got the only key."

"Smartarse."

The door clicked and Gabriel was left alone with his racing thoughts. And throbbing cock. Suddenly he regretted asking to have his hands bound. It was all very well and good for an anonymous double fuck, but it made wanking *really* difficult. He fidgeted anxiously, imagining how it would feel. Ryan and Daz had shared him, but not both in the same end at the same time. He'd done threesomes before, but never front and back at once. How would they do it? Would he straddle Aled's lap, because Daz didn't like tits? Or would it be the other way around, because Daz loved kissing him until his brains dissolved?

It seemed like an age before the door opened again. He heard four feet enter. The door click shut and lock. A hand wrapped around his ankle and pulled, and as he was tipped back into the bed, two more cupped his face and kissed him. Daz. The unfamiliar mouth. The taste. The way he was sealed shut like he couldn't breathe even as the kiss was gentle. That was the way Daz kissed and Gabriel melted.

The kiss broke. Hands vanished. The bed dipped behind him. He was turned, poked and prodded into a kneeling position — then the hands began to play with him. And mouths. His own was left alone, but there were lips on his neck. His left tit was massaged in a big hand and his right gripped by hungry teeth. A slick finger slid into his arse with a prickle of discomfort. Dry ones had no such qualms about his vagina and worked their way into the space left behind by the sex toy from most of his evening.

It was —

Gabriel gasped when the exploration turned into preparation. The squirm and wriggle of fingers both front and back was strange. His first climax felt like a deliberate ploy, rubbed out briskly and his breath barely steadied before his cunt was empty and his hips were taken in two hands. He was raised, still reeling, and came down so hard on that first prick that it was a shock. He flinched, jarring the hand that had never left his arse, and had his nipple twisted in punishment. As the sharp burst of pain faded away, he realised that two hands were spreading his cheeks and a third was pulling on his oversensitive cock.

And there was a cock pushing at his arse.

The breath was driven out of him as the first inch forced its way inside. Pain shivered through him as he felt the strange sensation of two living, beating things inside of him *touching*. He sagged forward.

And in doing so, figured it out.

In the familiar contours of the shoulder under his head. In the softness of the hands that bracketed his ribs. In nudge of lips against his ear. The whispered request for a colour. The flickering pulse of a cock inside of him that had paused for a moment.

Aled.

He was encompassed in Aled's hold. Aled controlled the room. Aled controlled *him*. He could smash Gabriel to pieces, here and now. He could take it all too far and drive the fantasy away under pain — real pain — and blind fear. He could twist Gabriel up like a half-chewed sweet and spit him out again.

"Green," Gabriel whispered.

Because he wouldn't.

Because he couldn't.

Because this was Aled — fucking him with a stranger because Gabriel wanted to try it, holding him like he was priceless even as two dicks worked inside of him in a rhythm that was dizzying and distracting, touching him like a maestro with a Stradivarius and not a man with a self-proclaimed whore…

Gabriel caught a slip of flesh between his teeth and held on.

He didn't need it—but he wanted it. He wanted Aled. Daz was good, but he was barely there. It was all Aled. His hands, his hair, his soft chest, his familiar smell.

Aled-Aled-Aled.

Gabriel breathed in deep as someone bottomed out, and exhaled, settling into the man who held him like snow into a mountain pass.

Right where he belonged.

Chapter Twenty-Two

"I now pronounce you man and wife."

The church burst into applause. Someone burst into tears. Suze flung her arms around a bawling Tom's neck and kissed him full on the mouth and Aled wasn't ashamed to wipe away a couple of tears of his own.

"Ladies and gentlemen, please rise for Mr and Mrs Hooper!"

The church rose in a cacophony of noise. The married couple set off back down the aisle to jubilant music, and the flash of what seemed like a million phones. Aled slid out of his pew and held out an elbow for Gabriel's hand to slide into the gap.

"You did good," Gabriel whispered and Aled grinned. He'd not dropped the rings. He'd not bawled too badly. All he had to do now was look decent in some photos and not fuck up his speech. Piece of cake.

And the box in his pocket was burning a hole.

The wedding photographer was Tom's sister-in-law, and bouncing around with a bright smile and endless instructions. Groom's family. Bride's family. Friends of groom. Friends of the bride. Fusty old female relatives. Racist male ones. Everyone in a stupid hat. Everyone who'd ignored the colour scheme. Now for people who clearly didn't understand what formalwear was. Now for a lovely shot with everyone here under the delusion there was a free bar. Aled smiled and posed, posed and smiled throughout a series of formal shots, then broke away for a quick kiss off to one side while the staff started to usher everyone down towards the dining room.

"Do I get to steal you yet?" Gabriel whispered.

Aled glanced up the corridor. He could do it now. He didn't want to make a scene at his best friend's wedding. They could step out, he could say his piece, it could be over and done with in just a few moments.

But he didn't want to just steal a couple of moments. He wanted more.

"Not yet," he said, "but I don't have to sit up at the high table."

"How did you talk your way out of that one?"

"I told Tom," Aled deadpanned.

Gabriel laughed.

Dinner was a fancy affair, much like his own wedding. For all her anxiety and neuroticism right up until she'd put her pseudo-dress on that very morning, Suze *glowed*. Speeches were funny. His own was a success. The ferocious mother-in-law cracked a smile or two. The photographer stopped bouncing and started taking natural shots. Aled slipped her a twenty to preserve one of him and Gabriel sharing a sweet, natural kiss over cake.

It was perfect.

It brought back memories of his own wedding without the tinge of sadness at its ultimate failure. It made him smile to see Suze so happy, without any sense of loss for her being so far away now. Gabriel's acerbic cynicism made him laugh and the easy willingness to stand up and sway with him when the dance floor was cleared and the smoochy music played made the laughter soften into a warm contentment simmering away low in his stomach. When Gabriel broke away to get a drink, the contentment stayed — but something stronger pulled on Aled's blood like there was a whole new version of gravity between them.

"Aled?"

The light touch on his arm made him jump. He turned to find Tom smirking at him.

"Go and tell him."

"Tell him what?"

"That you love the bloody earth he walks on. Come on, mate. If you can't do it at a wedding, when can you?"

Aled smiled and patted back.

"Go and grab your wife, and start it all off on the right foot," he said.

Then he broke away. Because what else could he say? Tom wasn't idle like Aled had been. He wouldn't take Suze for granted like Aled had taken Melissa. He didn't need Aled's advice. He was a good man and he'd make a good husband and a great dad.

Aled's life wasn't pointing that way anymore.

Out in the hotel gardens, dusk was falling. The party was winding down and guests beginning to drift away. The candles were burning down and the sky above them was crystal clear and studded with stars. It was, Aled thought, almost romantic.

And it was now or never.

He took a deep breath, patting his pocket and the box within it, and went to seek out his wayward partner. Suze's uncle, a deeply boring old bastard with a conservative streak so wide that he regarded Tom as 'one of them foreign types' for being from somewhere south of Birmingham, had taken a surprising liking to Gabriel based entirely on their mutual affection for cycling, and had accosted him at the bar to talk bicycle clips or puncture repair kits or whatever else it was that cyclists liked to talk about. He'd been doing it all afternoon and Aled hadn't minded.

But now, with the stars sprinkling a warm sky and the music turned down to a melodic hum designed to make the booze-fuelled guests tired and go to bed, Aled decided it was time and went on a rescue mission.

He found them by the empty buffet table, Gabriel nursing what looked like a vodka and what Aled was sure was the world's longest-lasting mouthful of water, and made a display of affection so obvious that Mr Taylor's face screwed up in confused disgust.

"Come on, babe," he said, nuzzling at Gabriel's ear for good measure. "Time we called it a night."

Gabriel came willingly enough, making polite apologies and smiling despite Mr Taylor's obvious and rapid reassessment of this rather excellent outdoorsman into one of them nancy types, but frowned when Aled took him out into the gardens and under the starlight.

"This isn't bed," he said, then grinned and wrapped his arms around Aled's neck. "Or did you mean a different type of calling it a night?"

Aled chuckled and unwound them. "I figured you might need rescuing."

Gabriel smirked. "Think you might have given him a coronary with that. He kept hinting it was a shame Suze didn't end up with a nice young man like me."

"She's a bit too fond of dick, it does have to be said."

Gabriel sniggered and turned to lean his elbows on the low wall around the terrace and stare out over the darkening gardens. "God, it's beautiful."

"Ye—"

"If you dare follow that up with a blatant pass at me, I'll slap you."

Aled laughed, mimicking Gabriel's pose and bumping their shoulders together lightly. "All right, all right. Even though it would be a *true* pass."

"Shove off."

"Love you too, petal."

Gabriel snorted, and Aled bit his lip, staring up at the stars.

"I do, you know," he murmured.

Gabriel made a faint sound and bumped back. "Yeah, I know."

"No, I mean—I *do*. I really do love you, Gabe."

"I know that, too."

"Do you?"

Gabriel paused, and Aled heard him shift. "Aled? What's the matter?"

Aled exhaled heavily. "This whole wedding—hell, the whole lead up to it, never mind tonight—has had me thinking."

"About your own wedding?"

"Yeah, in part."

"So—"

"Let me just…word-vomit."

"Um, okay."

"It's had me thinking about you and me. I was looking at Tom and Suze and thinking how I easily love you as much as Suze loves Tom, so why in the hell had he popped the question and a big gesture from me is still bringing you cheese on toast in bed?"

"But I *like* cheese on toast in bed."

Aled half-smiled at the almost petulant tone and tucked his forearm over Gabriel's to wind their fingers together, staring at those empty, ring-free fingers. God, Gabriel would look so beautiful wearing a ring, but —

"But the more I thought about proposing to you, the more terrified I became. Because rationally, I know my marriage would have collapsed in the end anyway, if we couldn't get around the issue of children, but I also know that I'd let it crumble enough to make Melissa's choice easy for her. I got complacent. I took her for granted. I had a woman I loved more than life itself, and I took it for granted that she'd always be there. Until one day she wasn't. And if I'd worked at it, kept working, not let a marriage certificate and a ring make me think she'd always be there, then maybe she wouldn't have left. Maybe I would have been enough to her still to make her hesitate, to make her decide that maybe she didn't need a baby, or maybe she would have cared enough to stay and chip away at me until I came around to the idea of adoption."

Gabriel squeezed his fingers silently and Aled blew upwards into his hair.

"Marriage means something to me," he said quietly. "I'm a traditionalist like that. If you love someone, really love them, then you marry them. You prove it to them, to your families, to the whole world, that you're this unit and you're never going to be separated. It's not just a piece of paper to me, but *because* it's not, I let it change the way me and Melissa worked. I stopped bringing her flowers and arranging surprise dates. I stopped bringing her cheese on toast in bed. I mean, you know, metaphorically, she wasn't much of an eating in bed person as you are—"

Gabriel snickered, his fingers tightening around Aled's again, and Aled smirked briefly.

"So I got caught up in this tangle, this 'oh, grow up, you learned your lesson, you won't make the same mistake with Gabriel' then following it right up with 'but what if you *do?*' And I couldn't take not doing it, because you're not just my boyfriend and someone to play with, you're so much *more* than that, but…I couldn't stand the idea of doing it, either, because if I fucked up again like I did with Melissa, I'd lose you. And…I—I can't go through another divorce and survive it, Gabe. I can't."

"Hey—"

"And with my dominant tendencies, God knows how I'd respond to existing in a marriage where I'm constantly terrified I'll fuck it up and you'll walk. I don't want to be that guy, Gabe. I don't want to be that guy who's so scared his husband will leave that he gets jealous of any hint of attention elsewhere, that he starts drawing unreasonable lines in the sand, that he ends up pushing his partner away because of his own issues."

"Maybe you wouldn't."

"I can't take that risk, Gabe. And I wouldn't ask you to do it, either."

"But—"

"So I'm stuck," Aled interrupted. He felt very hot, despite the night drawing in, and he knew he was flushing a violent red. "I want to propose, but I'm terrified of it."

"Er…well…"

"And in the end, I decided…"

"Aled." Gabriel sounded faintly alarmed.

"Just—just here," Aled said, and fumbled the box out of his pocket. Gabriel, in the candlelight, looked very pale, and Aled thrust the box into his fingers, curling them around it until Gabriel came back to life and held on for himself. "Open it."

"Aled, I—"

"Please."

Gabriel swallowed and opened it.

And his face, that pale, slightly scared look, changed. "Oh. *Oh.*"

"I can't do it, Gabe," Aled confessed in a rush. "I can't handle being married again and all the risk that comes with it. Because you and me, right now, we're exactly how I want us to be. But I don't want you to ever think, even for a minute, that I don't love you enough to marry you. Because I do. You're my world, and sometimes other people share that world, and that's fine by me, because all they get is a glimpse. They're tourists. I get the full view of just how brilliant and beautiful you are, and the way we are, I remember to work at it. I remember to tell you, I remember to make a fuss sometimes, I remember to—to bring you cheese on toast. So…it's not a ring. It'll probably never be a ring. But it reminded me of you and it's something you can play with when you're twitchy and I can't be there to cuddle you like you need, and I want you to wear it all the time, so you always remember me saying this."

"*Aled.*"

Aled finally looked up from their joined fingers and was met with a clumsy kiss landing half on his mouth, half on his chin. The charm—a simple dark sapphire set in silver, strung on a simple black string to hide nonchalantly under Gabriel's shirts — dangled from its cord, tangled in Gabriel's fingers, the fancy box abandoned on the wall.

Aled hadn't known quite what to say, or how to say it.

But he'd been heard all the same.

Want to see more from this author?
Here's a taster for you to enjoy!

Best Behaviour
Matthew J. Metzger

Excerpt

By the time Jim swallowed his pride, he was standing on the pavement with three bin bags and an overgrown spider plant.

"Can you come over?" he asked. "I need your help." Then he hung up.

Sarah rang back, of course, but Jim didn't answer. He just sat down on one of the bags, put the plant down next to his boot and leaned back against the railings.

Fuck.

That was the only thing that came to mind. *Fuck.* How the fuck had he ended up—well, no, he knew exactly how he'd ended up like this. Stupidity and pride and a whole host of other things that weren't all that flattering. And yet, even as he combed through them all in his head, he'd not change any of them. So, what did that make him?

At least it wasn't raining.

Stretching out his legs in front of him, Jim examined his tatty boots and absently wondered if he ought to try building sites. But even they needed certificates and shit these days. Only thing Jim knew how to do was put boxes on shelves and say, "Would you like fries with that?"

And even the places that sold fries didn't want him.

It wasn't that he hadn't tried. They'd known for months that the warehouse was going to fold eventually, and he'd been looking for other work. But everywhere asked for qualifications. And the places that didn't took one look at his history — specifically that weird little gap after that night with the car — and told him to get packing.

Well, he was packed now.

Whole life in three bin bags. And a plant. Great success he'd made of himself there. Wouldn't Mum be proud?

He snorted. No doubt Sarah would pass the message along.

He wanted nothing less than to have to ring Sarah, but he was out of options. If he ended up in a cardboard box on the streets — or, worse, a Sally Army hostel — then he *would* end up back in prison. Knew it just as much as he knew the sky was blue. And even his pride wasn't so huge as to want to go crawling back in there.

Still —

He'd had a plan, when he got out. Sort himself out. Get a job, find a flat, settle down with the right eight or ten people he'd like to shag for the rest of eternity. Sounded easy, when there were several hundred odd days to think about it in a cell. Only the right person hadn't been right after all. And the job hadn't lasted. And the flat needed the job.

Chewing on a corner of his thumb, Jim sighed. At least the bailiffs wouldn't be on first name terms with him anymore.

A silver Merc came creeping around the end of the road. It looked absurdly out of place in Jim's road full of burned-out Clios and old Skodas with black alloy wheels. It shimmered like a police car as it inched toward him and stopped right across the entrance to the flats as if it owned the lot of them. Driver probably could have *bought* the lot of them.

Jim lifted a hand and waved.

The driver's door opened. A ridiculously tall heel landed on the potholed tarmac and a slim woman unfolded herself from the car. She frowned down at him like a scolding parent or a disappointed probation officer and Jim could have laughed. She looked more like either of those than what she was.

"Hey, sis."

"What happened?" Sarah asked.

She didn't greet him. She certainly didn't hug him. Strip back all the pretence and they would have looked very alike — both tall, both with honey-coloured hair, both with the glass-cutting jawline. But Sarah's hair was in a perfect bun, her suit pristine, her nails gleaming. She hadn't even been working today, but that was how a mum of three *could* look when she hired a nanny. Then there was Jim — hunched over, hands in pockets, hair on end, unshaven, still wearing his hi-vis vest and dirty jeans as if he had a job.

Like peas in a mile-long pod.

"Lost my job," he said.

"Again?"

"We all did," he said defensively. "They've closed the warehouse."

Her frown eased a fraction.

"Then came home and the landlord was here. Said if I couldn't cough up five hundred by Friday he'd evict me. So I told him about the job, and" — Jim gestured to his spider plant — "here I am."

There was a long, long silence.

So long, in fact, that ice ages came and went. Evolution spawned four hundred new species. Mars underwent a century of its own. The big bang began to revert into the big crunch.

Then Sarah said, "Why did you owe your landlord five hundred pounds?"

"And the rest."

"What?"

"I owed him a grand and a half."

Her jaw dropped. "You *what?*"

Jim shrugged.

"Why weren't you paying your rent!"

"With what?" Jim asked. "They cut the gas off last week. I owe water like…four hundred and something. Even the bank's started threatening with bailiffs. I'm out of options. Why d'you think I rang you?"

Her jaw was still agape, but she spluttered.

"Four hun—the bank—*bailiffs*?"

"Yeah."

He felt about an inch tall and his stomach was clenching up. He was too hot. His leg started to jiggle.

"Why didn't you ask me for help?"

"I did. Am."

"Sooner than being—you've been evicted!"

The hot feeling boiled over. "Right. Yeah. Because asking worked so well last time."

"That was different."

"It really wasn't," he replied tightly. "That was *worse* than this."

She pursed her lips, eyeing his spider plant. It looked sorry for itself on the grubby flagstones. But to hell with her and her demands. She hadn't helped when he'd asked the first time. Why would he ask again?

"I tried everything," he said. "But today was the last straw. So here I am."

"Here you are," she echoed weakly, then shook herself. "Right. Well. Our spare room it is."

He grimaced but said nothing. The truth was, Jim didn't want Sarah's help or Sarah's spare room. He'd tried everyone else while the landlord had been flinging his things in the bin. Old work colleagues who didn't want to know. An ex-boyfriend who'd asked, "Who?" as though Jim had vanished out of existence when they'd split up. He'd even tried Justin, much as he didn't want to be around that smug fucker with his new fiancé.

But, in the end, nobody had been able — or wanted — to help.

So here he was, squinting up at Sarah in the dying light.

"Come on," she said. "Let's get that lot in the boot."

She didn't touch the bags. She just opened the boot and held the plant on her hip like a baby as he moved them. The smackheads over the road were staring and he flipped them off as he banged the lid down.

"Jim! This is a new car!"

"Sorry," he muttered.

"Let me just call Anthony…"

Jim rolled his eyes, unable to help himself. "I'm sure this'll go down really well."

She raised an eyebrow. "Don't you go bringing him into this."

"Why not?" he asked. "You brought him into it last time."

"It wasn't like that."

"Really, because it sure felt like that."

"Well, it wasn't."

Jim rolled his eyes but gave up. He wished he could end arguments like that. He wished his interpretation of events was the definitive one. What it must be like, to have that kind of power? But then he'd never had that power with Sarah. He doubted anyone ever did.

He let himself into the passenger seat as she talked on her phone and sulked in the front like a little kid. His skin itched. His stomach was a lump of lead. He desperately didn't want to be doing this — but it was just temporary, he told himself. Just until he could find another job. A better job. Longer hours and higher pay.

It was a short chat. She waved her hands a lot. And eventually she hung up and got into the driver's seat, mouth tight as though they'd argued.

"Told you he wouldn't like it."

"Enough, please."

Jim shut his mouth and stared at the flats as Sarah turned the car around, and they slowly vanished in the wing mirror.

"I didn't realise things had gotten this bad. You should have talked to me."

Jim grunted.

"You should have talked to Mum."

"Oh, right, yeah —"

"She's just worried about you."

"She screens her calls. She won't answer. Hasn't since I came out."

"I'm sure she —"

"Don't tell me what Mum means," Jim said tightly. "You weren't there. You didn't hear her. I know exactly what she means."

An uneasy silence fell between them. Sarah clenched and relaxed her fingers around the steering wheel in an anxious rhythm, and Jim's leg was jiggling again.

"How good did you think it was?" he asked quietly. "I'm eight grand in debt and I worked minimum wage. What did you think was happening?"

"I don't want to talk about that," she snapped.

It was all she'd ever said since that original no. She didn't want to talk about it. She never wanted to talk about it. If Jim brought it up, she changed the subject. Left up to Sarah, they'd *never* talk about it.

"I would have helped if you'd told me," she said after a while and Jim snorted.

"Since when do you *help?*" he demanded.

She pursed her lips. "Since always. You were just too stubborn to see it."

His jaw ached and he realised that he was grinding his teeth again. Slowly, he relaxed his jaw. He couldn't afford to piss her off now. He'd have to be on his best behaviour, at least until he found another job.

But it was a mutinous silence. Because the rub was that Sarah had been right. Anthony had refused to help because he was a judgemental prick, but Sarah had done this pragmatic refusal that had hurt worse, somehow. Religious bigotry, Jim could kind of roll with that. Anthony was dumb as his dog collar anyway — what did Jim expect?

But Sarah? Sarah's practicality had *hurt.*

And, worse still, it had been *right.*

So he seethed quietly as they left the city behind. The traffic was busy, commuters rushing home from their better jobs to their better homes with their partners and kids, not their sisters and crap in-laws. He stared out at the sea of other people as they inched away to the south and wondered if he'd ever get on track. Sarah had only four years on him, but she had it all figured out. Jim...Jim felt as if he'd been careering from one disaster to another ever since he was a kid.

And bleeding away into the wide avenues, long driveways and conservatories of Dore and Totley didn't help. Sarah fitted in out here. Her Merc, her suit, her manicure drumming ceaselessly on the leather. Jim felt like he had in prison and sank lower and lower in his seat as they left even the outskirts behind and dipped into the countryside proper.

The house lay just shy of the Derbyshire border — Jim could just about see the sign — and the electric gates were a foreboding barrier against the likes of him. The place screamed money. Gated drive. Detached twin garage. A summerhouse visible round the side. Since Jim had last been — when Agnes was born, over a year ago now — they'd had an honest-to-God fountain installed in front of the steps that led up to the front door.

It was more like a mansion than someplace people actually *lived.*

"It's been a while," he said uselessly as Sarah tucked the Merc into the garage next to a gleaming BMW on the latest plates.

"Yes."

"How's everyone?"

"Oh, they're fine."

Another long pause. Jim lifted his bin bags. Sarah took the plant. Then he was looking up at the house and he wanted to scream.

"Come on," she said. "I'll show you which room you can have. And you'll join us for dinner, won't you?"

"Not really that hung —"

"Of course you will," she interrupted as she opened the door. A bell chimed. "Zoe! Zoe, are you in?"

Jim was listening.

He stood in the hall and stared at the spiral stairs sweeping away to the first floor like something out of a wedding brochure. At the marble floor. At the chandelier. At the two-storey windows dominating the back of the hall and showing the gardens falling away to the south of the house. At the money oozing off the walls — and at the white dog collar, sitting proudly on a hook by a collection of tidy coats and above a rack of expensive shoes.

Forget Zoe. Anthony was home.

And this was going to be hell on earth.

PUBLISHING

Sign up for our newsletter and find out about all our romance book releases, eBook sales and promotions, sneak peeks and FREE romance books!

About the Author

Matthew J. Metzger is an asexual, transgender British author juggling books, an office job and a love of travel with the human need for sleep once in a while. He writes both adult and young adult books focusing on LGBT+ characters and their relationships, particularly those from the less salubrious areas in which he was dragged up over the years.

On the very rare occasions that Matt isn't writing, he can usually be found at the gym, halfway up a mountain or collecting new tattoos. (And yes, he does have book ink...)

Matthew loves to hear from readers. You can find his contact information, website details and author profile page at https://www.pride-publishing.com